William A. Woodworth

Descendants of Walter Woodworth of Scituate

William A. Woodworth

Descendants of Walter Woodworth of Scituate

ISBN/EAN: 9783337391607

Printed in Europe, USA, Canada, Australia, Japan

Cover: Foto ©Andreas Hilbeck / pixelio.de

More available books at **www.hansebooks.com**

ADDENDA.

Since the "Descendants of Walter Woodworth" was printed, Mr. Frank P. Woodward, of Malden, Mass., has unearthed the last Will of Walter Woodward, of Scituate, coming upon it quite by accident among the records of deeds in Plymouth County, Mass. It is a very important discovery, and it is unfortunate that it did not come to light in time to adjust the Woodworth Genealogy in conformity with it. The following is the Will and Inventory:

Will of Walter Woodward.

In the name of God, Amen. I, Walter Woodward, of Scituate, in the jurisdiction of New Plymouth in New England, in America, being weak in body, but of sound and perfect memory, praise to Almighty God for the same do make this my last will and testament in manner as followeth:

First, and most principally, I commend my soul into the hands of Almighty God, my creator, in and through Jesus Christ, my only Saviour and Redeemer, and my body unto decent and buriel at the discretion of my executors with the advice of the rest of my sons hereafter named.

And my temporal estate I dispose of as hereafter followeth:

Imprimis. I give and bequeath unto Thomas Woodward, my eldest son, a parcel of upland containing acres, lying in Scituate aforesaid, bounded by the lands of Henry Ewell on the south and the Common on the north, to be enjoyned to him and his heirs forever

Item: I give unto my two sons, Thomas and Joseph, acres of Marsh land, to be equally divided between them, which lyeth by Sussons—bounded by the Marsh of Anthony Collimer on the east, by the Marsh of Thomas Clap, deceased, on the north, in Scituate aforesaid to be enjoyned to them and their heirs forever.

Item: I give to Thomas Woodward, my son, one-third part of

all my land at Seconet, which I purchased. The other two-thirds I give unto my two sons, Benjamin and Isaac Woodward, to be equally divided between them, to be enjoyned to them and their heirs forever, excepting twenty-five acres, of which I do give unto my son Joseph, to be enjoyned to him and his heirs forever. Ten acres of which I do give unto my daughter, Martha, to her, her heirs forever, of which two quantities of land is to be deducted out of the two-thirds of my land lying at Seconet given to my two sons, Benjamin and Isaac aforesaid. All the rest of my land at Seconet, which is yet to be purchased, I give unto my two sons, Thomas and Joseph Woodward, to be divided equally between them, to be enjoyned to them and their heirs forever.

Item: I give to Benjamin, my son aforesaid, my dwelling-house with my barns and other outhousing, with all my land, both upland and marshland thereunto belonging, that is to say, twenty acres of upland, be it more or less, bounded by land of John Turner to the west and by land of Joseph Otis to the east, and six acres of marshland more or less bounded by the land of Joseph Otis to the northeast, and by the first herring brook towards the south--all of which said housings and land with all the appurtenances thereof, the commons and privileges thereunto belonging I give to the said Benjamin, my son, his heirs forever, always provided upon condition that my son, Benjamin, aforesaid, do pay and allow the sum of seventy pounds unto my son, Joseph, and my six daughters, Sarah, Elizabeth, Mary, Martha, Mehitabel and Abigail, ten pounds apiece, to be paid to them at three payments, viz., one-third part of the said seventy pounds to be paid to my said children within three years after my decease and the other two-thirds to be paid in the two following years, that is to say--in each year a third of the said sum of seventy pounds, and each payment to be paid, the one-half in silver and the other half to be paid in corn; and (cattell?). Further, my will is that my son Benjamin, aforesaid, do allow my two daughters, Mehitabel and Abigail, the lower room or parlor at the northeasterly end of my dwelling house aforesaid, for their use during the time they do live unmarried.

Item: I give and bequeath unto my said two daughters, Mehitabel and Abigail, my feather bed with the furniture thereunto belonging, and all the rest of my household goods I give unto my six daughters, Sarah, Elizabeth, Mary, Martha, Mehitabel and Abigail, to be divided equally among them. The rest of my estate undisposed of by this my last will and testament, I give and bequeath to all my chil

dren, all my debts, funeral expenses being first paid, to be equally divided amongst them.

Item: I do constitute and appoint my son, Benjamin, aforesaid, the sole executor of this my last will and testament, whom I do appoint to pay all my debts and legacies and I do appoint my two sons, Thomas and Joseph Woodward, overseers of this last will and testament.

In witness whereof, I have hereunto set my hand and seal the twenty six day of November, 1685.

The mark of—
WALTER X WOODWARD.

Signed, sealed and acknowledged in presence of—
THEO. KING, Senior,
THOMAS PALMER,
CHARLES STOCKBRIDGE.

Thomas King, Senior, Thomas Palmer, Charles Stockbridge, the witnesses to this above said will, appeared before the Court and gave oath that they, the said above Theo. King, Senior, Thomas Palmer and Charles Stockbridge, did see Walter Woodward above said, sign, seal and deliver this instrument to be his last will and testament, taken before the Court March 2d, 1685-6.

Attested to—
NATHANIEL CLARKE,
Secretary.

AN INVENTORY of all and singular goods, lands and chattels of Walter Woodward, of Scituate, late deceased, taken by us whose names are hereunder written:

ITEM.

In purse, and apparel and books	05	10	00
In one bed and furniture	05		
In one bed and furniture	04		
In bedding	02		
In one brass kettle and warming pan	02	05	
In one iron pot	00	12	06
In one dripping pan and peeler		06	
In one enamelled frying pan and tongs		08	
In one cupboard	03		
In one table	01		
In one set work, cubs or tubs V spinning wheel	01	10	
In one bedstead and three chairs		02	
In chests	00	03	

In hemp sheep wool and yarn....	03	15	08
In four cowes	10		
In one oxen and three young cattell..............	06		
In two sheep	00	10	00
In forks, loges (not decipherable) and iron hoops....		07	
In one-third part of chairs?........................		05	
In 12 bushels Indian corn..........................	01	16	
In dwelling-house and barn and upland and meadowland adjoining thereto, with common privileges	140		
In ten acres salt meadowland......................	50		
In five acres upland................................	20		
In one whole share of land in Seconet..............	100		
	£355	10	

SAMUEL CLAP,)
JOHN WILLIAMS.)

Benjamin Woodward appeared before the Court and gave oath that the above-written is a true inventory of his late father, Walter Woodworth, deceased, so far as he knows, and when more comes to his knowledge, he is to bring it to this inventory by virtue of the oath in Court, March 2d, 1685-6.

(Attest)

NATH'L CLARKE, Sect'y.

It will be observed that the name is spelled Woodward, except in the oath of Benjamin, where it is spelled Woodworth. The transition from one name to the other seems to have been remarkably easy in those early days.

This Will makes necessary an entire reconstruction of the numbering of this genealogy. From the will it appears that Thomas and not Benjamin was the eldest son and should therefore be No. 1 instead of No. 3. The relative standing of the other sons cannot be determined from the will. As to the daughters, however, it may safely be inferred that they are mentioned in the will in the order of their age, especially as they are named twice in the same order. The dates of birth of Mary and Elizabeth are given in the Scituate records; Mary born March 16th, 1650; Mehitable, Aug. 15, 1662. The dates of marriage of Thomas, Benjamin, Joseph and Martha are also found in the town records. Assuming then that

they were then at least twenty-one years of age, we are enabled to construct the family of Walter as follows:

1 Thomas, born about 1636, married about 1666.
2 Benjamin, born about 1638, married about 1659.
3 (Walter, born about 1645, married about 1669.)
4 Joseph, born about 1648, married about 1669.
Mary, born March 16, 1650, married Dec. 24, 1677.
Martha, born about 1656, married June, 1679.
5 Isaac, born about 1659, married about 1686.
Mehitable born Aug. 15, 1662.
Abigail, born about 1664, married (Dec. 21, 1695).

An important point to be noticed is, that the will makes no mention of a son Walter. The inference should not, however, be hastily drawn that he had no such son. The Little Compton records mention a Walter, who has been assumed to be the son of Walter, Sr., although it is no where so stated in direct terms, except by Dean, in his history of Scituate. According to the Little Compton town records, Walter was born 1645, married 1669, and had children, Joseph, born 1670, etc., as stated on page 15. The records of the United Congregational Church, of Little Compton, mention Walter born 1669, Joseph or Walter baptized 1672, Benjamin, 1674 and Isaac, 1676. It is quite evident from the failure to mention the day and month of births and marriages, that these entries in the town records were not contemporaneous with the events, but were made at a later date at the request, perhaps, of some descendant, who had only an indefinite general impression of the facts. The dates of death are more specific, and very likely the entry of births was then first made. These entries are therefore not entitled to the implicit confidence which would otherwise be accorded to them. There are also other circumstances which have tended to throw a doubt upon the reliability of these records. For instance, it is stated that Walter's child Hezekiah was born 1672; Catherine, 1673, and Benjamin 1674. Such a rapid fecundity is, to say the least, very improbable. Then again, some of the children mentioned may easily be accounted for by giving them to other known sons of Walter. Joseph, born 1670, bap. 1672, married 1691, may be son of Joseph 4, who was born March, 1670, and married 1694 (p. 61). Hezekiah, born 1672, may be the son of Thomas 3, born 1670 (p. 53). Catherine, born 1673, may be the daughter of Thomas 3, born Oct. 5th, 1673 (p. 53). Benjamin, born 1674, may be the son of Joseph 4, born Aug., 1676 (p. 64). Isaac, born 1676, may be the son of

Walter, Sr. (p. 7), who must, however, have been born as early as 1660. Elizabeth, born 1678, may be the daughter of Joseph, born 1680 (p. 6); but Thomas, born 1680, is not so easily accounted for.

Thomas (p. 53) was married about 1711 and had five children born at Little Compton and the dates of their birth are specifically given in the Little Compton records. No other Thomas can be found in Little Compton or Scituate, to whom this family can be assigned.

These palpable errors and suspicious coincidences, however, do not seem to be sufficient reason for entirely ignoring both the town and church records. They are still entitled to some degree of credit; indeed, the correspondence of these independent records of the town and the church is strong proof of their general reliability. The fact that Walter, Sr., does not mention any son Walter in his will is not conclusive proof that he had no such son. He does not mention his wife, but it is nevertheless true that he had a wife who was the mother of his sons. She was undoubtedly dead at the time Walter made his will in 1685. So the failure to mention his son Walter may be accounted for on the hypothesis that he also was dead at that time. This supposition is not contradicted by any of the Little Compton records, where Walter last appeared in 1680, when his son Thomas was born. There is, however, this statement in the Plymouth Colony records: "Recorded and admitted as Free men at ye General Court, held at Plymouth on the first Tuesday of June, 1689. Joseph Woodworth and Welter Woodworth, of Scituate," according to which there was a Walter in Scituate four years after the death of Walter, Sr.

There is, however, a serious difficulty about Benjamin, whom I have made son of Walter, Jr. (23), which I am not able satisfactorily to dispose of. It does seem certain, however, that I have erred in making him the Benjamin mentioned on page 18, who settled in Lebanon in 1703. Benjamin, of Lebanon, died 1728, leaving a will dated Jan. 21, 1728, in which he mentions fourteen children, all of whom, except possibly Ezekiel and Caleb, were then unmarried. The last of them, Amos, was born in 1773. If they were all 21 years of age at the time of their marriage, then Amos was born in 1702 and the others prior to that; putting the births of the 12 children two years apart, we must run back to 1678 as the latest date of the father Benjamin's marriage. It is clear then that this could not be the Benjamin, son of Walter Jr., who was born about 1674.

The newly discovered will of Walter, Sr., makes it quite probable that Benjamin, of Lebanon, was the son of Walter, Sr. By this will Walter, Sr., devises to Benjamin and Isaac a one-third interest of his lands at Seconet or Little Compton, after deducting 35 acres for Joseph and Martha. In the deed of lands at Lebanon to Benj. in 1703, he is described as "Benjamin Woodworth, of Little Compton, R. I." Moses, son of Isaac, after his father's death in 1714, conveys to Benjamin "of Lebanon" 5 acres at Little Compton, "being one third part of a lot of 15 acres, originally Walter Woodworth's." These circumstances are straws indicating the identity of Walter's son Benjamin with Benjamin of Lebanon. There is this difficulty, however, which is a very serious one. Dean says: "Benjamin was a soldier in King Philip's war and lost his life. Lands were assigned for his services to Charles Stockbridge for the use of Benjamin Woodworth's family in 1676." There are so many errors in Dean's History that this statement might be disregarded, except for the fact that it is corroborated by the town records of Scituate (book 5, p. 200), where it appears that on July 21st, 1676, Charles Stockbridge was appointed to receive lands for the family of Benjamin Woodworth killed in King Philip's war, and at a later date a deed was executed by the town to Benjamin's son Robert. The will of Walter, however, by which, in 1685, nineteen years after King Philip's war was ended, he devises land to his son Benjamin, and the oath of Benjamin, in 1786, to the inventory of his father's estate, effectually dispose of this difficulty.

But again, Dean further says, "he" (Benjamin), "had daughters Elizabeth, Deborah, Abigail (wife of John Jackson, of Plymouth, 1695), and a son Robert, who settled in the west part of the town, east of Symonds Hill, where Dominick Bowker now resides. His children were Ruth, born 1695," etc., as appears in the Scituate records compiled on page 8 of this genealogy. None of these children, except Deborah and Elizabeth, are mentioned in the will of Benjamin of Lebanon. This difficulty might be avoided in two ways—first, on the supposition that Abigail and Robert were dead at the time Benjamin made his will; or second, on the assumption that these children remained at Scituate instead of emigrating with the rest of the family to Little Compton and Lebanon, and that their father Benjamin had already amply provided for them, by settling upon them the Scituate property, which had come to him through his father's will.

Since writing the above, Mr. Frank E. Woodward has written me that he is satisfied that Benjamin had two wives, the first Deborah, by whom he had Elizabeth, Deborah and Mary. She died, and pre-

vious to Benjamin's settling out in Scituate in 1691, he had married Hannah, by whom he had the rest of his children. These statements are borne out by church records of the second parish of Scituate. Abigail was not the daughter of Benjamin at all, but of Walter, Sr. Dean has got matters very much twisted. Robert is unaccounted for either in the town or church records.

It must be confessed that these facts taken together are somewhat mystifying. It is noticeable, too, that, while the names and dates of birth of the children of Thomas and Joseph, who lived in Scituate, are recorded in full in Scituate records, and the names, etc., of the children of Walter, Jr., and Isaac are recorded in the Little Compton records, there is no mention in either of the children of Benjamin. Benjamin evidently lived in Scituate prior to his father's death, for his father gives him the homestead there and makes Benjamin his executor and Benjamin takes on himself the execution of the will there. Robert must have been born about 1663 to 1664; the others probably before Walter's death. Why is there no record of these births? Is it possible that there was another Benjamin, who was killed in King Philip's war and who was the father of Robert, Elizabeth, etc., but was not the son of Walter? If so, who was he, and where did he come from? Or shall we yet come into possession of facts which will reconcile all these apparent contradictions and inconsistencies?

WM. A. WOODWORTH.

White Plains, N. Y., June 9, 1898.

DESCENDANTS OF

WALTER WOODWORTH

OF SCITUATE, MASS.

Descendants of Walter Woodworth, of Scituate, Mass.

The following record of the WOODWORTH family is very far from complete, and a large outlay of labor and money will be necessary before it can be made into anything like a finished genealogy. When the work of compiling this record was begun in 1878, the author was acquainted with only one family of the name of WOODWORTH except his own and therefore supposed the task would be a light one. But no sooner was the search begun than the WOODWORTHS began to buzz about in countless swarms, and it soon appeared that the family was not so scarce as it was modest. The ramifications of the family were found to be so widely spread throughout the United States and Canada that it was impossible for any one without abundant leisure to devote all his time to the work, to trace them all out. The author has given a large part of his leisure time for the last twenty years to the compiling of this record and although its incompleteness is evident, the facts that its records have been carefully verified and the author believes it to be accurate so far as it goes, and at the urgent request of many of the family he has concluded to publish it with the hope that at a future day a sufficient number of supplemental facts may be gathered to make a larger and more complete history possible.

The first mention of the name WOODWORTH in this country is found in the records of the town of Scituate, Mass. Scituate adjoins Plymouth on the north and was settled in 1628, eight years after the landing of the Pilgrims in the neighboring town, by "men of Kent" England. Among them was WALTER WOODWORTH, and there are reasons for the belief that he was the first WOODWORTH in the world. A search in the records of the County Kent England, in 1628 and prior, fail to disclose the name. The name WOODWARD, however, is found there and it is possible, indeed quite probable, that WOODWARD was the original name and through some process of evolution became WOODWORTH. It is certain that many of WALTER'S decendants were called WOODWARD and held that spelling

to this day. MR. FRANK E. WOODWARD, of Malden, Mass., who has given much study to the WOODWARD branch of the family, is very firm in the belief that the original name was WOODWARD, which, as he puts it, became "corrupted" to WOODWORTH. It would have been more grateful at least if he had said "improved;" certainly even he cannot deny that the latter is a more "worthy" name. Woodward meant a keeper of the wood. In this new land where all woods were free, such a name was meaningless and smacked of feudalism and tyranny; hence WALTER, who had turned his back on all such things, very naturally wanted a change and adopted the name WOODWORTH, though some of his descendants seem to have backslided into the ways of royalty again and resumed the discarded name of WOODWARD.

There has been no discovery of a WOODWORTH in any of the early settlements of this country prior to WALTER of Scituate. Mr. W. G. Woodworth, a very old gentleman residing at Centerville, St. Joseph Co., Mich., claims to have been descended from BENJAMIN WOODWORTH, who came from England with his brother William and settled in Salem, Mass., two years after the landing of the Pilgrims, and the tradition further goes that WALTER, their younger brother, came over with his wife some years later and settled in Scituate. No record, however, of any such WOODWORTHS can be found in Salem, although a large number of WOODWARDS appear on the town books. It may be that the "corruption" to WOODWORTH came later to the family of Benjamin of Salem, than to that of WALTER. This branch of the family, if such it is, will be only incidentally referred to in this narrative, as there is not yet sufficient data to identify it.

Mr. E. S. Woodworth, of Windham, O., (see 411418) gives us the following ingenious theory to account for the name WOODWORTH. He says that the original ancestor of the family was one Silas Wood, who, on his voyage from the old country to New York, fell in love with a fellow passenger, a young lady of the name of Worth. This lady was possessed with a settled determination never to change her name, but taking kindly to the addresses of Silas, she finally consented to marry him on condition that he would blend his name as well as his heart with hers. Silas was not slow to accept this condition, and the name WOOD-WORTH was the result. The story is certainly a very pretty one, and is entitled to be enrolled in the family mythology.

Another story altogether different and yet strangely enough emanating from a cousin of the above named E. S. Woodworth, the Hon. Laman G. Woodworth, M. C., of Youngstown, O., (411162) is that the first ancestor was named WOODROFFE or WOODROUGH and came over in the Mayflower and our honorable kinsman corroborates his story by speaking with

pinned" to a gimlet, in his possession which this ancestor brought over with him. Unfortunately for this story there was no person of either of those names who ever came over in the Mayflower, unless he took passage as a stowaway.

The WOODWARD family in the United States is very numerous and comes from several distinct sources. The name is found in the earliest records of Boston, Salem, Watertown, Scituate, Taunton and elsewhere, indicating early settlers from the mother country. There was a HENRY WOODWARD, who came over in the ship "James," in 1635, and settled in Dorchester, whose name is frequently spelled in the early records, Woodworth, and he may have been a brother of WALTER WOODWORTH, of Scituate. He was the ancestor of a large family, some of whom afterward settled in Lebanon, Ct., where many of the descendants of Walter had made their home. And in the Lebanon records there appears, in 1719, the name HENRY WOODWORTH, who was undoubtedly a descendant of HENRY WOODWARD and a son of JOHN WOODWARD and Ann Dewey, born March 18, 1650, at Lebanon. In Scituate we find the names of the descendants of WALTER spelled variously WOODWORTH, WOODWARD, WOODARD, WOODART. Among an unlettered people devoted to agriculture and busy in their leisure hours defending themselves against the Indians little attention was paid to niceties of spelling and pronunciation so long as the identity of the individual was preserved. The name WOODWORTH is a little difficult to pronounce and it came much easier to say WOODRUFF or WOODARD or WOODWARD—we have all been through with that experience even in these later days—and thus there came at last a new spelling and the evolution of a new name and perhaps the complete obliteration of a family as WOODWORTHS. In like manner it is probable that many WOODWARDS have become WOODWORTHS; possibly, too, there has been a similar mixture with the WOOLWORTHS and WOODRUFFS. On this account a great deal of confusion has arisen and there has been great difficulty in making these researches to keep the families distinct.

The following record is confined almost exclusively to those families which have retained the name WOODWORTH and no special effort has been made to follow out the departures and deviations, although some such deviations are noted in cases where they were easily ascertained.

I am indebted for much valuable assistance in compiling this record to George W. Woodworth, of St. Louis; C. C. Woodworth, of Rochester; James S. Woodworth of Worcester, Mass., Frank E. Woodward of Malden, Mass., Dr. Beschir, of Boston, and Albert B. Woodworth, of Concord, N. H.

The method of numbering is simple. Each male is numbered in the order of his birth from 1 up, and to this number is prefixed the numbers of all his ancestors. The sons of WALTER the first are numbered from 1 to 5, and

[illegible] are respectively [illegible] the same manner, each [illegible] father's number prefixed. For instance, WALTER'S son BENJAMIN is numbered 1. BENJAMIN'S son ROBERT is numbered 11, and the [illegible] sons are numbered respectively 11, 112, 113 and so on from generation to generation; so that it can be seen at a glance to which branch of WALTER'S family any [illegible] belongs. For instance, ZIBA 5323 is descended from ISAAC 5, from ISAAC'S third son DANIEL 53, from DANIEL'S [illegible] son BENJAMIN 532, while ZIBA himself is the third son of BENJAMIN and is therefore numbered 5323.

WALTER WOODWORTH probably came from Kent, England. There is no absolute proof of this statement, but it may be reasonably inferred from the well-authenticated fact, as stated in Dean's History of Scituate, that Scituate was settled by "men of Kent." The religious nature, which in a marked manner has characterized his descendants, may be accounted for by the probability that for ages the WOODWORTH family had breathed the religious atmosphere of Canterbury Cathedral, where perhaps an early ancestor had listened to the preaching of St. Augustine and received into fruitful soil the first seeds of Christianity, which in later years became disciplined and strengthened by the austerity of Thomas a Becket. It is a noticeable fact, however, that the great majority of WALTER'S descendants are Dissenters, and, among a considerable number of clergymen, none are Episcopalians.

It is not likely that our family "came over with William the Conqueror." We do not find the name enrolled among William's knights at Battle Abbey. The name as well as the physical and intellectual characteristics of the family are Saxon rather than Norman. But the origin of the family must, for the present at least, remain a matter of conjecture. Behind Scituate the veil of the Atlantic is drawn and our ancestry is lost in the mist of bygone ages.

To WALTER WOODWORTH in 1635 was assigned the third lot on Kent street, which runs along the ocean front, at the corner of Meeting-house lane, and there he built his house. In 1675 he appears to have owned other lands, a tract on the First Herring Brook not far below Stockbridge Mill, where afterward stood the residence of the poet, SAMUEL WOODWORTH, and another tract on Walnut Tree Hill just west of the [illegible] Greenbush or South Scituate R. R. Station, which was, in early times, called Walter Woodworth's Hill; and in 1666 he becomes the [illegible] of 60 acres at Weymouth. In 1640 WALTER was assessed 9s "for the public use." March 2, 1641, he was admitted as a freeman, and on June [illegible] 164[illegible] he was appointed surveyor of highways in Scituate, and again in 1646 and 1656. His name appears frequently on the town records of Scituate [illegible] juror, [illegible] and in the performance of other public duties. In 1654 he was a member of the First Church, which ordained Charles Chauncey as [illegible]

manner, but he [illegible] of the [illegible] kind, although he enjoyed it as much as some of the more [illegible] Puritans. However much he may have been in his personal living, WALTER'S love of peace and good-will to men had its limitations, for when his next door neighbor, Japhet Turner, in 1671 pulled down WALTER'S fence and obliterated his boundary lines, WALTER promptly sued him and obtained a verdict for £5 and costs. The moral effect of this verdict was healthy and stiffened up the backbone of his children, all of whom became successful and respected citizens. His daughter, Mehitabel, is mentioned as having been "unfortunate as to her health." She was afflicted with some nervous disorder, which in those superstitious days was synonymous with being "possessed with the devil;" in other words, she was under the influence of witchcraft and Mary Ingham was charged with being the witch. On March 6 1676, she was indicted in the following language:

"Mary Ingham, thou art indicted by the name of Mary Ingham of the Town of Scituate, in the jurisdiction of New Plymouth, for that thou, having not the fear of God before thine eyes, hast by the help of the Devil in a witchcraft or sorcery, maliciously procured much hurt, mischief and pains unto the body of Mehitabel Woodworth, the daughter of WALTER WOODWORTH, of Scituate aforesaid, and some others; particular causing her, the said Mehitabel to fall into violent fits, and causing great pains unto several parts of her body at several times so as she, the said Mehitabel Woodworth hath almost been bereft of her senses and hath greatly languished to her much suffering thereby and the procuring of great grief, sorrow and charge to her parents—all which thou hast procured and done against the law of God and to His great dishonor, and contrary to our Sovereign Lord the King, His crown and dignity."

Mary was tried and acquitted and thus an end was put to the nonsense of witchcraft in the town of Scituate.

WALTER left no will and there is no record as to the name of his wife, but the names of his children are found in the town records of Scituate:

Children of WALTER WOODWORTH—

1 Benjamin believed to be the eldest

2 Walter, b 1645.

3 Thomas.

4 Joseph.

Mary, b Mar. 10, 1650, m Dec. 24, 1677, Aaron Symonds, of Green-field.

Martha, m Lieut. Zachary Damon, June 167[illegible].

5 Isaac.

Elizabeth, unmarried.

M[illegible]ble, b Au[illegible] 1[illegible] 1662

1 BENJAMIN was a [illegible] in King Philip's War, [illegible] he was killed, and as a [illegible] to his family, lands were assigned [illegible] Chark [illegible] Stockbridge in trust for them. In the deed afterwards made of this [illegible] to Benjamin's son Robert, the name is written WOODARD. His children were—

1 Robert, b 1660.

Elizabeth, m Oct. 1[illegible]7, to Thomas Chittenden.

Deborah.

Abigail, m Dec. 21, 16[illegible]5, to John Jackson, of Plymouth.

11 ROBERT, b 1660, at Scituate, married and settled in the western part of Scituate, east of Symond's Hill, where Dimirick Bowker resided in 1831. Robert and his children have their names spelled in the town records invariably, WOODARD. His children were:

Bertha, b Dec. 5, 1685; m Benjamin Tower May 6, 1718.

James, b Jan. 25, 1687-8; d Feb. 17, 1691.

1 Benjamin, b May 31, 1690.

Elizabeth, b Aug. 23, 1692.

Joanna, b Feb. 20, 1694.

2 Robert, b April 15, 1697.

Mary, b April 27, 1699.

Deborah, b May 11, 1701.

Ann, b May 4, 1704.

Lydia, b Sept. 3, 1706.

3 James, b Aug. 9, 1709.

111 BENJAMIN WOODARD, m Mary Wright Aug. 17, 1712. She was born in 1691, and died soon after the birth of her child, Benjamin, who was b Dec. 18, 1713, and d young. BENJAMIN married for his second wife Anna Torrey, Feb. 14, 17[illegible]. Her children's names are spelled in the records, WOODWORTH.

1 Benjamin, b Feb. 26, 1717.

2 Joseph, b July 20, 1720.

Anna, b April 7, 1722, m John Soper, Oct. 13, 1743.

1111 BENJAMIN WOODWORTH, b Feb. 26, 1717, m Hannah Cudworth Jan 27, 1742.

Children—

1 Benjamin, b 1750

Anna, m Mr. Johnston.

Ruth, m Mr. [illegible]ardell, 17[illegible].

11111 BENJAMIN, b 175[illegible], m Abigail Bryant Nov. 14, 1778. Deane, in his history of Scituate, says this Benjamin was the son of JAMES 1[illegible].

but [illegible] is [illegible] that [illegible] had [illegible] and settled in Maine. His children born in Scituate were—

Abigail or Nancy, b Jan. 31, 1780, m Wm. Russell.

Amos, b Oct. 23, 1781, moved to Detroit in 18..

1 Benjamin, b Dec. 29, 1782.

2 Samuel, b Jan. 13, 1784.

BENJAMIN married for his second wife, Betsy, widow of Capt. Joseph Northey, of Scituate. He was a Revolutionary soldier and was in the Battle of Dorchester Heights in 1775. He died Aug. 7, 1830, at the old Norway place, half a mile south of the old Stockbridge Mill.

111111 BENJAMIN, b Dec. 29, 1782, at Scituate, learned a carpenter's trade at Boston, and in 1804 went to Detroit, where he became enterprising, popular and prosperous. He ran the first stage coach in Michigan, built the first brick house in Detroit, and for many years kept the best hotel there. He served in Capt. Lindley's regiment in the war of 1812. In 1841 he lost a large amount of property by fire and then removed to St. Clair, Mich., where he lived in peace and quiet with his only surviving daughter, Frances, until Nov. 10, 1874, when he died at the age of 92. He was popularly known all over the State of Michigan as "Uncle Ben." He married Rachel Dicks, of Detroit. His children were—

Abigail, m Charles W. Ewing, Fort Wayne, Ind.

1 Samuel D.

Ann Maria, m Gen. S. B. Brown, St. Clair, Mich.

Frances Elizabeth, m A. J. Cummings, St. Clair, Mich.

Ruth, Louisa, Catherine, Mary Catherine L., Benjamin, Henry and James all died young.

A daughter of Abigail, Mrs. L. A. Bond living at Fort Wayne, to whom I am indebted for much valuable information respecting this branch of the family, writes: "I have reason to be proud of my ancestors; to be sure in the long run, poverty instead of wealth were theirs, but they were always possessed of honesty and nobleness of character, which are by far greater treasures than riches."

Frances Elizabeth, m Andrew J. Cummings, hotel keeper, St. Clair, Mich. They had five children, Fannie, Ida, Louisa, Mary, Lena.

1111111 SAMUEL D., m Lucinda Allen, and lived at Monroe, Mich. He was killed by a boiler explosion on the old steamer "Vance." He had one child—

1 Benjamin R.

11111111 Benjamin R., m Jennie Taylor, of Detroit. Served as Lieut. in

the army during the Rebellion and died of consumption contracted there. He left one son—

1 Charles C. T.

111112 SAMUEL, b at Scituate, Jan. 13, 1784, m Lydia Reeder Sept. 23, 1810. Early in life he learned the printer's trade at Boston and devoted much of his time to writing verses. In 1809 he removed to New York and established a weekly newspaper. His literary taste brought him into contact with the noted authors of the time and in 1822, he, together with Geo. P. Morris and afterwards with N. P. Willis, began the publication of the "New York Mirror." He was the author of the famous poem, "The Old Oaken Bucket," the delightful freshness and rhythm of which makes it one of the cherished gems of our American literature:

THE OLD OAKEN BUCKET.

How dear to this heart are the scenes of my childhood,
  When fond recollection presents them to view.
The orchard, the meadow, the deep tangled wildwood,
  And every loved spot which my infancy knew;
The wide spreading pond and the mill that stood near it,
  The bridge and the rock where the cataract fell;
The cot of my father, the dairy house nigh it,
  And e'en the rude bucket which hung in the well.
The old oaken bucket, the iron bound bucket;
  The moss covered bucket which hung in the well.

That moss covered vessel, I hail as a treasure;
  For often at noon, when returned from the field,
I found it the source of an exquisite pleasure,
  The purest and sweetest that nature can yield.
How ardent I seized it, with hands that were glowing!
  And quick to the white pebbled bottom it fell;
Then soon, with the emblem of truth overflowing,
  And dripping with coolness, it rose from the well.
The old oaken bucket, the iron bound bucket,
  The moss covered bucket arose from the well.

How sweet from the green mossy brim to receive it,
  As poised on the curb it inclined to my lips;
Not a full blushing goblet could tempt me to leave it,
  Though filled with the nectar that Jupiter sips.

And now, far removed from the loved situation,
The tear of regret will intrusively swell,
As fancy reverts to my father's plantation,
And sighs for the bucket which hung in the well;
The old oaken bucket, the iron bound bucket,
The moss covered bucket, which hung in the well.

He wrote also "The Hunters of Kentucky," "Zoological Jurisprudence," "Quarter Day, or the Horrors of the First of May," "Champions of Freedom; a History of Our Late War;" a number of songs and ballads; a drama, "The Forest Rose," and many other poems (which, some few years ago were republished by Scribner & Co.). He became one of the most popular poets of a day when New Yorkers delighted to exalt local names and native literature. He became much enfeebled during his later years in consequence of a paralytic stroke. His last poem, which was found among his papers after his death, but is not found among his published poems, was a quaint descriptive poem entitled "The House I Live In," which is especially interesting for the local history of New York City, which it records, rather than for its literary merits. The poem contains 27 verses of which the following will give an idea of the style:

"Our city then did not extend
Beyond the Collect Brook,
And one might, from its northern end,
Upon the Battery look.
Broad street was but a muddy creek
And banks were very few.
The Greenwich stage ran twice a week
When this old house was new."

The last stanza of this poem gives an insight into the poet's heart:

"But though my sight be dull and dim,
My Saviour's love was prized,
In youth I placed my hopes in Him,
And now they're realized.
Yea, though He slay me, still I'll trust;
His promises are true;
Though this old house decay, He must
Rebuild it good as new."

He died at his home in New York Dec. 9, 1842. His old home at

S[illegible] is still [illegible] of the North[illegible] Ry., about five minutes walk from the [illegible] Station. The old well is there but the old oaken bucket has yielded to modern improvements; the bucket is reputed to have come into the possession of Rev. Daniel Wright, of South Scituate, who died in South Natick a few years ago.

SAMUEL'S children were:

1 Samuel Smith Haines.
  Harriet Mansfield, d unmarried.
2 Selim Edward
3 Frederick Augustine.
  Georgianna Louisa.
  Caroline Matilda.
  Lydia Huntley.
4 Benjamin Russell.
  Mary Josephine.
  Maria Juliana.

1111121 SAMUEL S. HAINES, usually called Haines, which was the name of his mother's grandfather, married Orpha Reeder in 1839, at New York. He died in New York in 1844. Had 3 children—

1 William, d in California in 1868.
  Julia, m John Conner, California, had 7 children.
  Louise, m Wm. Parkinson, Orange County, N. Y., has 4 children.

1111122 SELIM E., b in New York Nov. 27, 1815. He was an adventurous youth and spent much of his time at sea. He embarked in 1834 on the ship Margaret Oakley and was wrecked off the coast of Madagascar. He was rescued by the natives and lived for some months among them, but eventually escaped and returned home. He entered the navy as midshipman in 1838 and in 1862 was promoted to be the Commander for gallant service under Farragut. He spent the latter part of his life at San Francisco, Cal., where he became very popular. He died Jan. 19, 1871. SELIM'S widow, ten months after her husband's death, married Erasmus Dennison, a young naval officer, ten years her junior, a son of Gov. Dennison, of Ohio. He committed suicide two years later, leaving his widow and one child now residing in San Francisco, Cal. Selim left 5 children—

1 Selim, in the navy.
2 Frederick, b 1858; entered the Naval Academy in 1872; stood second in his class of 170. Was suspended for hazing; and though after-

wards [illegible] never returned, but went [illegible] resides with his aunt, Mrs. Whit[illegible], in Brooklyn.

3 Benjamin lives in San Francisco.

4 William lives in San Francisco.

Lydia lives in San Francisco.

5 Samuel.

FREDERICK A., a highly accomplished man, "idol of the family," died at San Francisco Feb. 2, 1865, unmarried, leaving a large estate.

Daughters of SAMUEL (111112)—

Georgianna m Watts Beebe in 1840. He died in 1861 leaving two daughters.

Georgianna afterward married Theodore Schell, who died in 1877. They had 7 children, 3 of whom are dead; one, Lucy, married Wm. Edwards, of San Francisco, and has 5 children.

Caroline, d in California, 1885, unmarried.

Lydia, m Wm. Cooke Nov. 22, 1844, d 1857, leaving children—

Lydia, b 1846.

Carrie, b Aug. 4, 1849.

Minnie, b Dec. 23, 1851, m a son of Admiral Selfridge, U. S. N., San Francisco.

Belle m Sylvester Sibley, Chicago, 3 children.

Willie, m, lives at Syracuse, N. Y.

Mary J., m James S. Wethered, of Baltimore, Aug. 21, 1860, resides in Brooklyn, N. Y. Children—

Levina, b April 29, 1861.

Carrie, b Aug. 9, 1862.

Molly, b Aug. 31, 1864.

Woodworth, b Aug. 9, 1866.

Julia, m Joseph McArthur, a graduate of West Point, who served in the Civil War and was retired as Major. She died in 1874, leaving 4 children, Selim, Lewis, Benjamin and Julia, all residing in Chicago.

BENJAMIN, son of Samuel, the poet, embarked at Hong Kong for San Francisco in 1861 and was never again heard from. The vessel was lost at sea.

1112 JOSEPH, b May 2[illegible], 172[illegible] at Scituate m Sarah Jones Oct. 7, 17[illegible].
His children were—

1 Joseph, b June 14, 1746.
Sarah, b May 12, 1749.
Anna, b June 17, 1851.
2 James, b June 17, 1754.
Hannah, b Sept. 6, 1757.

I have found no other trace of the descendants of this family. The above children were all born at Scituate.

---

112 ROBERT, b April 15, 1697, at Scituate, m Deborah Sylvester in March, 1719; I find no further trace of him.

---

113 JAMES, b Aug. 9, 1699, at Scituate, m Sarah Soper Dec. 6, 1731. His name is spelled WOODART, WOODWARD, WOODARD on the Scituate records. His children were—

1 James, b Sept. 17, 1732, d single.
Lydia, b Aug. 21, 1734, d single, 1815.
Sarah, b March 25, 1736, d young.
Bethia, b Jan. 23, 1737.
Sarah, b April 14, 1740, m Shearjashub Bourn, d 1819.
Mary, b May 14, 1742, m John Wright, 1769.
2 Joseph, b June 6, 1744.
3 John, b June 6, 1746.
Elizabeth, b 1748.

Sarah, wife of JAMES, d 1748, and JAMES m again Feb. 15, 1749, Mary Stetson, widow of John Vinal, Jr.; she was a daughter of Anthony Stetson, and was born Dec. 9, 1717. Their children are—

4 Samuel, b Oct. 9, 1750.
5 William, b July 12, 1752.
6 James, b Aug. 12, 1754.
7 Elisha, b Sept. 27, 1756.
8 Benjamin, b Oct. 7, 1758.

Dean's history makes the James who married Mary Stetson to have been the son of JAMES 113. This is evidently a mistake as the will of James, Sr., dated Sept. [illegible], 1775, and proved Nov. 16, 177[illegible], mentions the name of his wife Mary, as well as the above-named children. He signs his name "James Woodart," and thenceforward this branch of the family seem to have adopted the name "Woodard, now "Woodward."

1131 SAMUEL, b [illegible], at Scituate, removed to Bristol, Me.

1135 WILLIAM WOODARD, b July 12, 1752, at Scituate, m Mehitable Bead and removed to Bath, Me. Children--

Rhoda, m Jan. 30, 1805, Wm. D. Whitmore.

Rachel, m Bailey Jenkins, Scituate.

Elizabeth, m Abel M. Donnell.

1 William, m Hannah Sprague.

2 Ezra, m Bethia Brown.

The remainder of this branch of the family, which reverted to what was the original name, WOODWARD and corrupted to WOODARD, has been carefully studied out by Frank E. Woodward, of Malden, Mass., who has published the results of his researches in the Maine Historical and Genealogical Record.

2 WALTER, b 1645, at Scituate, m 1669, at Little Compton, R. I., where he and others of the family bought lands. Dean says "Walter" (son of Walter, Sr.), left children--Mary, b 1658, Mehitable, b 1662, Ebenezer, b 1664." This is manifestly wrong, as it would make Walter to have married at the tender age of 12. Mary and Mehitable were probably the children of Walter, Sr. Who the Ebenezer spoken of by Dean was, I cannot say; he may have been a son of Walter, Sr., or he may have been a son of Thomas 3. The Little Compton records contain entries of Walter's birth and marriage as above, as well as the following minutes of the birth of the children--

1 Joseph, b 1670, m 1694 (no further trace).

2 Hezekiah, b 1672.

Catherine, b 1673, m Thomas Davenport July 20, 1704, d June 1, 1728.

3 Benjamin, b 1674.

4 Isaac, b 1676.

Elizabeth, b 1678, m Benjamin Southworth Dec. 18, 1701, d June 18, 1712; had 4 children.

5 Thomas, b 16[illegible].

12 HEZEKIAH, b 1672, at Little Compton, m Hannah Clapp Dec. 23, 1697, d Nov. 23, 1716. She d Dec. 10, 1734. The following children were born at Little Compton--

1 Elisha, b Dec. 1, 1698.

2 Elihue, b July 24, 1700.

Samuel, b March 25, 1701, d May 28, 1705.

Deborah, b Nov. 17, 1703, d Aug. 28, 1733

Hannah, b March [illegible], 17[illegible].
Mary, b March 4, 17[illegible], d July [illegible], 17[illegible]

I assume that HEZEKIAH was the son of Walter 2, though he may possibly have been the son of Thomas 2, born at Scituate 167[illegible] and adopted into the family of Walter after the destruction of Thomas's house at Scituate—see HEZEKIAH 31.

221 ELISHA, b at Little Compton, R. I., Dec. 1, 1698, m first Jane Bailey, of Scituate, May 10, 1722. She was b 1701 and d Feb. 6, 17[illegible]. Second, Ann Clapp, May 17, 1730. Elisha d at Little Compton April 20, 1749.
1 Hezekiah, b Dec. 1, 1732.

2211 HEZEKIAH, b at Little Compton, Dec. 1, 1732, m Abigail Southworth Dec. 13, 1753, d at L. C. March 22, 1761. His widow d Jan. 14, 1805. Children—
1 Elisha, b May 30, 1755.
2 Samuel, b 1757.
Esther, b 1759.

22111 ELISHA, b May 30, 1755, at Little Compton, m Edith Wilbour, daughter of Charles Wilbour, at L. C., Nov. 11, 1790, d July 17, 1827., at L. C. Children—
Esther, b July 14, 1791.
1 Hezekiah, b May 14, 1793.
Anna, b Feb. 28, 1794.
Abigail, b March 22, 1797.
2 Samuel, b Jan. 24, 1799.
Hannah, b June 30, 1801.
Lydia, b Nov. 8, 1803.
Sarah, b Nov. 8, 1803.
Mary, b Oct. 12, 1806, d Feb. 17, 1816.
3 Daniel, b Feb. 27, 1808.
Rachel, b Nov. 21, 1808.
4 Elihu, b May 7, 1814.
5 Elisha, b June 8, 1817.

221111 HEZEKIAH, b at Little Compton, R. I., May 14, 1793, m Rhoda Springer, daughter of John Springer, Dec. 27, 1819, d Feb. 17, 1864. Children—

1 Henry Staples, b Oct. 20, 1825, living at Providence, R. I., in 1890.
2 John Q. A., b Oct. 18, 1826, living at Providence, R. I., in 1890.

221112 SAMUEL, b L. C. [illegible] 179[illegible], m Dec. 31, 1821, A[illegible] Wilbour, b Sept. 4, 1804, daughter of Isaac Wilbour.

1 Charles, b Dec. 2[illegible], 1824.

Lydia Ann, b April 22, 1834.

221113 DANIEL, b at L. C., Feb. 27, 1808, m Mary [illegible] ——.

1 David Sylvester, b Aug. 5, 1830, at L. C.

Mary.

221114 ELIHU, b at L. C. May 7, 1814. No further trace.

121115 ELISHA, b at L. C. June 8, 1817, m Lydia Brownell Dec. 16, 1834, lives in Chase street, Fall River.

Lydia Maria, b 184—.

1 Elisha Edward, b Oct. 28, 1842.

22112 SAMUEL, b at L. C. 1757, d Jan., 1778.

---

222 ELIHU, b at L. C., July 24, 1700, m Silence Stoughton, of Dartmouth, Mass., March 6, 1727, d Sept., 1780. Children—

Mary, b Nov. 30, 1727.

Hannah, b Jan. 22, 1729.

Sybil, b Dec. 25, 1731, m Constant Hicks, of Dartmouth, Mass., March 4, 1752.

1 Thomas, b Aug. 3, 1734.

2 Stephen, b July 16, 1736.

Deborah, b Nov. 12, 1738.

Naomi, b Sept. 21, 1741.

Sarah, b April 2, 1744.

2221 THOMAS, b at L. C. Aug. 3, 1734, m Judith Briggs Sept. 12, 1755. She died at Falmouth, N. S., April 4, 1762. He had one child b in Scituate, Mass.

1 Job, b Feb. 11, 1757.

THOMAS emigrated to Falmouth N. S., in 1760, where his wife died April 4, 1762. He married again Margaret McCurdy, June 12, 1763. Children—

2 John, b Feb. 22, 1764.

3 Paul, b Nov. 3, 1765.

4 Thomas, b May 12, 1767.

5 Stephen, b Feb. 11, 1769.

6 Benjamin, b Nov. 28, 1770.

7 Joseph, b July 20, 1772.

Mary, b Aug. 12, 1774.

8 Alexander, b Jany 6, 1779.
9 Isaac, b Nov. 11, 1781.

BENJAMIN, b 1671 at Little Compton, R. I. In 1703 he bought for £220 from Philip Smith a large tract of land in Lebanon, Ct., where or in the neighborhood of which, many of his friends and relatives from old Scituate had settled. Benjamin moved to Lebanon soon after with his family; was admitted as an inhabitant Dec 22, 1701, and died April 22, 1728. There are no records either at Lebanon or Little Compton of the births of his children, but in his will executed Jan. 21, 1726, and proved June 20, 1728, his children are mentioned in the following order:

1 Benjamin.
2 Ichabod.
3 Ebenezer, b March 12, 1691.
4 Amos.
5 Ezekiel.
6 Caleb.

Deborah, m Sprague.
Hannah, m Walter.
Ruth, m Caleb Fitch, April 4, 1717.
Judith, m Thomas Newcomb, 1726, moved to Salisbury, Ct.
Margaret, m Joshua Owen, Nov. 5, 1718.
Priscilla, m Amos Fuller, June 29, 1721.

BENJAMIN'S farm was situated in the northeast part of the town and, on account of its remoteness from the church, we find in 1711 among the 24 signers of a petition for a new church, the names of Benjamin, Ezekiel, Benjamin, Jr., Ebenezer and Henry. Who Henry was I have been unable to learn, but the others are undoubtedly the children of BENJAMIN (25). In 1716 a new church was formed, called Lebanon North Parish or Lebanon Crank, and in 1804 this parish was cut off from Lebanon and made into the town of Columbia.

I also find the names of Ichabod, Ebenezer, Amos, Ezekiel and Ebenezer, Jr., mentioned in a rate bill for 1741 to pay the salary of Eleazur Wheelock, pastor, afterwards First President of Dartmouth College.

The farm of BENJAMIN is now in the possession of the Kingsley family, where it has been for four generations.

W. G. Kingsley, of Lebanon, Ct., who now resides on the old Benjamin Woodworth place at Lebanon, says:

"The will of Benjamin Woodworth of Lebanon, which was executed Jan. 21st, 172[illegible], contained legacies to his sons, Benjamin, Ichabod, Ebenezer, A[illegible], Ezekiel and Caleb, also to his daughters, Deborah Sprague, Hannah Walter, Ruth Owen, Judith Newcomb, Margaret Power and Priscilla Fuller. The property disposed of by this instrument covered his real and personal estate in Lebanon and also all his estate in the town of Seconet, in Mass. Bay, now Rhode Island. His son Benjamin was appointed executor. The will was proved June 20th, 1725, but by the record of our town he was in life until April 22d, 172[illegible]; therefore I think our record contains an error of at least a year concerning the time of the decease of Benjamin Woodworth."

231 BENJAMIN. The exact date of his birth is unknown; he was probably the oldest child, as he is mentioned first on the list of children in his father's will of which he was appointed executor. He was born probably in R. I., perhaps in Seconet, where his father owned lands. He married Mary Weeks July 20, 17[illegible], and died April 22, 1747, at Lebanon. Children—

Desire, b April 26, 1724, d March 11, 1728.
Elizabeth, b April 8, 1726.
Mary, b Oct. 27, 1727.
1 Benjamin, b June 8, 1729.
Desire, b Jan. 10, 1731.
2 James, b Oct. 11, 1733.
Hannah, b Dec., 1735.
Mercy, b Jan. 24, 1737.
Naomi, b May 22, 1739, m Elijah Hill Nov. 9, 1757.

2311. BENJAMIN, b June 8, 1729, m Mercy Swift July 19, 1750, had two children born in Lebanon. Served in Co. 4, Col. Durkee's Regiment during the Revolution; his name is found on the muster roll in 1779, where he is described as from Lebanon, age 50. Children—

1 William, b Feb. 7, 1751.
2 Swift, b Oct. 16, 1759.

2312 JAMES, b Oct. 11, 1733, m Hannah [illegible]ckstone at Lebanon, March 30, 175[illegible]. He was an ensign in the army during the war. His wife "amiable and beloved consort of Ensign James," d May 1, 1765, aged 27. He married again in 1765 the widow Mehitable Phelps, who died Feb 24, 1820, aged 8[illegible]. JAMES d Aug. 15, 1812. All are buried in the Columbia, Ct., burying ground. The children by his first wife are

Hannah, b Feb. 1[illegible], 1760, m Samuel Burnham Dec. 2[illegible], 1785.

John, b Nov. 21, 17[illegible], died young.
Children by his second wife—
Molly, b Nov. 23, 1767, m Ambrose [illegible], had 12 children.
Lucy, b Aug. 7, 176[illegible], m Asa [illegible], had 3 children.
1 James, b Nov. 23, 1770.
2 Samuel, b May 16, 1772.
3 Benjamin, b July 28, 1773.
Mehitable, b April 19, 1775, m Guy Robinson.
4 Alanson, b Aug. 25, 1781.

23121 JAMES, b Nov. 23, 1770, m Susannah Bailey; believed to have moved West.

23122 SAMUEL, b May 16, 1772, m Lavinia Babcock, believed to have moved West.

23123 BENJAMIN, b July 28, 1773, m Mary Marsh, of Lebanon, 1794; he d Sept. 24, 1856; she died Jan. 10, 1864, aged 86; both are buried in the Columbia, Ct., burying ground.
Children—
Jane.
Lucy, m ——— Hill, lives in Cal.
Nancy.
1 Henry, b about 1800.
2 Alanson, d, buried by the side of his parents.

231231 HENRY, b about 1800 in Columbia, Ct., m Clarissa Bingham, of New Hampshire, and removed in 1820 to North Carolina, where he died in 1840. In 1848 his widow moved with her children to Arkansas. She was a woman "eminent for her Christian virtues."

1 Henry, b 1825.
Mary, b 1829, m Edward Taylor, farmer, Ark.
2 Benjamin, b 1831.
Clarissa, b 1834, d Oct., 1878.
3 Sam. T., b 1836.

2312311 HENRY, b 1825 in N. C., now (1878) living in La.

2312312 BENJAMIN, b 1831 in N. C., now (1878) in La.

2312313 SAM T., b 1836, m 1863, Martha L. Armstrong; is manager of the W. U. Telegraph office at Victoria, Tex., and is also farmer and stock raiser. He offers to supply any member of the Woodworth family intending to start a menagerie with "horned frogs, free gratis, for nothing."

1 Louis Henry, b 186?.
Aurora W., b 1871.
2 Walter Bingham, b 1873.
3 Sam. Jr., b 1875.

23124 ALANSON, b Aug. 28, 1751, probably moved to western New York.

---

232 ICHABOD, b before 1700, took a "freeman's oath" 1716, m Sarab ——; he d Nov. 26, 1768; she d May 3, 1753, at Lebanon.

1 Lebbeus, b Jan. 8, 1723.
2 Silas, b March 22, 1725.
3 Jehiel, b Sept. 17, 1728, m June 6, 1751.
4 Reuben, b Aug. 22, 1738.

2321 LEBBEUS, b at Lebanon Jan. 8, 1723, m at Lebanon April 23, 1761, Anna Payne. He was a surveyor and constable; d at Lebanon, June 4, 1803. She died June 8, 1803. Children—

Anna, b July 19, 1762, m Abia Weed, of Brakamstead Ct., April 16, 1795.
1 Cyrus b May 4, 1764.
2 Ezra, b Aug. 5, 1765.

23211 CYRUS, b May 4, 1764, was a cadet at West Point and died there Sept. 22, 1781.

23212 EZRA, b Aug. 5, 1765, graduated from Dartmouth College in 1788; married Susa (or Sukey) Gage, Nov. 15, 1791; ordained a Congregational minister Jan. 18, 1793; was pastor of the Church at Winsted, Ct., afterwards at Madison, N. Y., and finally at Ludlow, Vt., where he died Sept. 11, 1836, aged 72. His wife d May 9, 1841, at Salem, N. Y. Children—

Susa, b June 27, 1794, at Winsted, m Jesse Walker, Madison, N. Y., Oct. 9, 1820; left two sons, Benj. F. and John H.
1 William Gager, b Nov 4, 1796.
Mary Ann, b Oct. 26, 1798, m Stephen Cummings, Ludlow, Vt., Sept., 1823.

232121 WILLIAM GAGER, b Nov. 14, 1796, m Sallie Simons, of Madison, N. Y., Feb. 28, 1821; d at Madison Feb. 22, 1828; she d Sept. 24, 1832.

1 Samuel Mills, b Jan. 3, 1822, d July 23, 1847.
2 George W., b March 9, 1824.
Jerusha Gager, b Nov. 4, 1826.

GEORGE W., b March 9, 18[illegible], m Mattie L. Reed, at Greenville, Mass., Oct. 25, 18[illegible], and had two children.

Florence E., b Dec. 22, 1868, at Cleveland, O.

Mattie L., b Jan. 1, 1875.

His wife, Mattie, d Jan. [illegible], 1879, and he married Oct. 11, 18[illegible], Anna H., daughter of Hon. Darius Lyman, of Ravenna, N. Y.

1 George Lyman, b Aug. 24, 18[illegible], at Geneva, N. Y.

GEORGE W. in 1881 resided in St. Louis and was connected with the "Puritan Gold and Silver Mining Co." 223 Olive street. He now lives in California. I am greatly indebted to him for much valuable information regarding the family, which he has worked up at considerable expense and trouble. Jan. 1, 1881, he sent out a circular letter of which the following is a copy:

St. Louis, Mo., January 1st, 1881.

Dear Friend:

Thinking it might be a satisfaction to know what progress I have made in tracing the ancestry of the Woodworth family, can now say that after spending much time corresponding with parties in this country and England and considerable money for copies of records, etc., I find they came from the County of Kent, England, and I have obtained a perfect record of that branch of the family to which I belong back to WALTER WOODWORTH, who settled in Scituate, Mass., about the year 1635, and to whom I think each party receiving this circular letter can trace his or her ancestry.

Tradition says two brothers (Woodworths) came to this country at an early date, one settling in New England, the other in New York, which I think connect many of the name known to me whose ancestry is traceable to New York. It is a pleasure to say that from the many letters received I find the Woodworth family possessed of more than average intelligence, and many of the names of prominent professional and business men enjoying a high reputation.

With the compliments of the season and many thanks for the aid afforded by you, I remain

Yours truly,

GEORGE W. WOODWORTH.

Geo. W. does not agree with Frank E. Woodward, of Malden, Mass., who, as we have before seen, claims that the name of the original Walter, of Scituate, was a Woodward. One of his strongest reasons being the fact that Walter is in almost every instance

2322 SILAS, b March 22, [illegible] at Lebanon, m Sept. 22 1746, Sarah, a daughter of Richard and Mary English. He emigrated in 1760 to Cornwallis, Nova Scotia, and is mentioned as one the of the grantees of [illegible] acres of land granted by George II., after the expulsion of the French. There are five Woodworths named in this list of grantees: Amasa, Benjamin, Silas, Thomas and William. SILAS d about Sept. 28, 1790. Sarah d May 23, 1805. Children—

1 Silas, b March 21, 1747.

2 John, b Feb. 17, 1749.

3 Solomon, b April 16, 1751.

4 Josiah, b July 10, 1753.

Sarah, b July 28, 1755, m Fred'k Babcock, d May 12, 1826.

5 Ezekiel, b April 11, 1758, d Sept. 1, 1759.

Elizabeth Seaborn, b May 21, 1760, on board the ship "Wolf," on the passage to N. S.; hence her name "Seaborn." She m Abraham Masters and d Aug. 1852, aged 92. She had ten children.

6 Richard, b Feb. 8, 1763.

7 Ezekiel, b Jan. 2, 1766, m Lydia ———; d Jan. 31, 1812, no children.

8 Eleazer, b Nov. 3, 1768.

23221 SILAS, b March 21, 1747, at Lebanon, m Zeruiah Bill Oct. 5, 1768, d June 14, 1776. They had one child.

Theodory m Feb. 20, 1786, Samuel Casey.

23222 JOHN, b Feb. 17, 1749, at Lebanon; went to Cornwallis, N. S., about 1760. Married Submit Newcomb Feb. 9, 1769. Children—

Hannah, b Sept. 11, 1769, m Joseph Pierce April 11, 1793; d May 21, 1821.

1 Ira, b Feb. 7, 1771, m Deborah Sanford.

2 Abner, b Jan. 19, 1773.

Sarah, b Oct. 29, 1774, d March 22, 1841, teacher, unmarried.

Alice, b April 12, 1776, m Stephen Chase Jan. 7, 1796.

Silas, b April ——, 1777, d soon of small pox.

3 John, b April 8, [illegible].

4 Benjamin, b Feb. 2, 1781.

5 Elias, b Sept. 7, 1782, d Sept. 20, 1879.

Elizabeth, b Sept. [illegible], 1784, m [illegible] B. Eels 1812.

6 James, b Aug. 10, 1786, m [illegible] 22, 18[illegible], [illegible] Fox.
7 Andrew, b Oct. 6, 178[illegible], m [illegible] Davidson and d 1870.
Submit, b May 1794, d young.
8 Solomon, b Dec. 15, 17[illegible].
Submit, b Jan. 4, 1796, m Thomas McGee, d 185[illegible].
Rebecca, b June 4, 1797, d Jan. 23, 1857.

JOHN d at Cornwallis, May 18, 1821. His wife, Submit, d May 29, 1816.

232221 IRA, b Feb. 7, 1771, m Deborah Sanford 1801.

232222 ABNER, b Jan. 19, 1773, m Hannah Loveless Feb. 23, 1797, at Cornwallis, N. S., d Sept. 3, 1859; she d March, 1856. ABNER m a second time when 87 years old and d within a week after.
John, b Jan. 31, 1798, d 1799.
Alice, b Jan. 14, 1800, d 1825.
Jane, b Aug. 3, 1802, d 1847.
Eliza A., b June 9, 1804, m W. H. Skinner Oct. 27, 1835.
Lydia, b Aug. 4, 1806, d 1856.
1 Solomon, b Aug. 25, 1808.
2 Francis, b Jan. 23, 1813.
Hannah, b Sept. 19, 1810, d 1838. (1835?)
Submit, b May 31, 1815, d Sept. 2, 1878.
Isabel, b Aug. 22, 1817, d May 15, 1872.
John H., b Feb. 15, 1820, d 1882.

ELIZA ANN, daughter of Abner, b June 9, 1804, m Wm. H. Skinner Oct. 27, 1835, lives at Somerset, Kings County, N. S. Children—
Alice, b Nov. 15, 1835, d 1837.
Hannah, b Jan. 12, 1837.
Wm. Albert, b Jan. 28, 1841.
Isabel, b May 7, 1843, d April 15, 1856.
John W., b Nov. 18, 1844.
Isaac, b May 27, 1846.
Rebecca, b May 27, 1846.
Sophie, b Jan. 29, 1850.

2322221 SOLOMON, b Aug. 25, 1808.
1 George N., youngest and only living son in 1880.

232223 JOHN, b April 5, 1779, at Cornwallis, N. S., m Margaret Bells Nov. 14, 1809. He d Nov. 1, 1827. Children—
1 William, b Oct. 13, 1810, not married.
2 John Bowles, b Sept. 5, 1812, m Mary A. Caldwell, d March, 1853.

Elizabeth Ca[illegible], b Aug. 2[illegible], 1814, m Hanson Chesley, Bra[illegible]ton. N. S.

232224 BENJAMIN, b Feb. 5, 1781, at Cornwallis, N. S., m Phebe [illegible] 1812. Children—

1 Enoch Lamaler, b Aug. 25, 1812.

2 Elias Ellis, b May 18, 1814.

3 John Samuel.

4 William Henry.

5 Charles Cowperthwaite, b Nov. 28, 1824.

232225 SOLOMON, b Dec. 15, 1793. blacksmith, m Margaret Alice Newcombe April 26, 1847. He was a ruling elder in the Presbyterian Church. He d Dec. 5, 1883. Children—

Edwin, b March 21, 1848, d May 7, 1857.

1 John Elihu, b May 10, 1849.

Mary Clarissa, b June 3, 1851.

Sarah Somerville, b Jan. 13, 1854, d May 13, 1857.

2322251 JOHN ELIHU, b May 10, 1849. He writes the following interesting letters:

Abstract of a letter from John E. Woodworth to George W. Woodworth, Esq.:

"The Woodworths came to Nova Scotia, at least to Kings County, from Lebanon, Ct., in 1760, and settled with others upon lands vacated by the deportation of the Acadians five years previously. The grant dated July 25th, 1761, of the township of Cornwallis, contains the names of five Woodworths viz., Amasa, Benjamin, Thomas, William and Silas. The last was my great grandfather; he married Sarah, daughter of Richard and and Mary English, of Lebanon, Ct. What relation the above-named five bore to each other I do not know. Their descendants are abundant in the township. I forward the names of some with whom I was acquainted who would be likely to be interested in your work, but the country is extensive and there are numbers of whom I know nothing.

"In reference to the first settlers and early inhabitants in America I think probably that John B. Newcomb, Esq., of Elgin (?), Kane County, Illinois, would be able to furnish you with much valuable information. He has compiled a genealogical memoir of the Newcomb family (published in 1874) and from correspondence which I had with him while it was in course of preparation I know that he preserved all the information which he could obtain concerning "collateral" families. If he is still living (I have heard nothing from him for four years) I know he would be delighted to assist you if in his power."

[illegible] Kings County, Nova Scotia, Jan. 2[illegible], [illegible].

Geo. W. Woodworth, Esq.

Dear Sir: Many thanks for your favor of Jan. 1st. I am gratified to learn that your efforts to trace our ancestry have resulted so satisfactorily. For my part I can only say that I think the family owe you a debt of gratitude, if nothing more. I supposed it was your intention to publish the result of your researches in a sort of Historical Memoir of the family in America but the tone of your letters does not confirm my suppositions. Something of the kind should be done and doubtless will before long.

In my former letter I think I gave the name of five Woodworths (from a list of the grantees of Cornwallis Township), who settled in Kings County about 1760. There was another, named Joseph, who came from Lebanon, Ct., and settled in Horton, Kings County. I knew his descendants, but I did not know the name of their ancestor when I wrote; supposed him to be one of the five named. Tradition says this Joseph was no relation to the others but was of Welsh descent. I doubt this although I fancy the family to be of Celtic extraction. My father's brother, Elias, was once accosted by a newly arrived British soldier, who was positive he had known him in Wales and that his name was Woodworth.

In reference to what you say about the New York Woodworths I may say that I think a branch of our family settled in that State. I have seen a letter, which I cannot find now, among my father's papers, dated Leyden, N. Y., 1820, signed Josiah Woodworth, and styling my father "Dear Cousin."

I am pleased to find that you have so high an opinion of the family; generally, so far as my acquaintance goes I believe that opinion to be well founded.

Repeating my thanks for the great service you have rendered the family and for personal favors, I am

Very truly yours,

JOHN E. WOODWORTH

———

SOLOMON, b April 16, 1751, at Lebanon, m Hannah Dewey July 26, 1772, d March 19, 1803. Children—

1 Daniel, b February 18, 1773.

2 Lodiz, b Aug. 16, 1774.

Lydia, b July 22, 1776, m Joseph Libby Dec. 5, 1812.

Sarah, b Jan. 16, 1780.

3 Silas, b Sept. 2, 1781.

4 Samuel Casey, b Dec. 6, 1787.

5 Charles, b Aug. 19, [illegible].

232234 SAMUEL CASEY, b at Cornwallis, N. S., Dec. 6, 1787, m July [illegible], 18[illegible], Hannah Masters, his cousin, daughter of Elizabeth Seaborn, daughter of Silas 2322. Children—

Catharine, b April 29, 1813.

1 Silas Newton, b Aug. 11, 1819.

Mary E., b Feb. 19, 1822.

23221 JOSIAH, b July 16, 1758 at Lebanon, m Anna Dewey April 17, 1783; lived in Ellington, Conn., till 1810, then moved to New York State where he d March 25, 1837. Children—

Caroline.

Sarah.

Hannah.

Anna.

1 Josiah.

2 Solomon.

232241 JOSIAH, b in Connecticut, lived in Leyden, N. Y. John E. (232[illegible]) writes that his father received a letter from Josiah in 1826, calling him "cousin."

23225 RICHARD, b at Cornwallis, N. S., Feb. 8, 1763, m Tamer Porter Oct. 9, 1783, d Sept. 1, 1796; she d 1802; they had two daughters and one son.

23228 ELEAZUR, b at Cornwallis Nov 3, 1766, m Mary Chute 1791, d July 5, 1844; his wife d Oct. 7, 1851. They had five sons and six daughters, whose names have not been ascertained, except two—

Charlotte, m John Sandford March 7, 1821.

Olive.

2323 JEHIEL, b at Lebanon, Sept. 17, 1728, m Phebe Collins June 6, 1751. Children—

Cyrenus, b March 6, 1752, at Lebanon, d soon.

Lucy, b Jan. 2, 1754.

1 Reuben, b Dec. 22, 1755.

2 Cyrenus, b Aug. 27, 1757.

Debbanie, b March 7, 1761.

23231 REUBEN, b Dec. 22, 1755, at Lebanon, Ct.; moved early in life to New York State and served in the Revolution as private, corporal and drummer in Capt. Ephraim Woodworth's 13th Reg't.

Children--
St. John.
1 Jewett.
2 Ambrose.
3 Esther.
3 Enos.
4 Henry.
5 Josiah.
6 Andrew Jackson, b April 29, 1833, m Lydia c VanWie Dec. 13, 1856.
7 Elias.

I have received no other information about this family than the following:

2323127 ELIAS, jobber, lives at Medford, Steel County, Minn., m Helen Van Wie Feb. 22, 1848. Children--

Jane Diadamia, b Sept. 9, 1849, m Jan. 1, 1871, Chauncey S. Carpenter.
1 Frank Day, b Aug. 2, 1854.
Lydia Christian, b July 8, 1857, m Oct. 19, 1876, A. L. Fowler.
Helen E., b Dec. 21, 1862.
Esther.
2 William E., b Aug. 20, 1866.
3 Frederick E., b Jan. 10, 1861.

2324 REUBEN, b at Lebanon, Aug. 22, 1733, m Elizabeth McGee Nov. 2 1757. Farmer, moved to Otsego Co., N. Y., in 1797.

1 Abel, b June 6, 1758.
Elizabeth, b Aug. 3, 1760.
Olive, b June 8, 1762.
Adah, b March 11, 1764.
2 Jehabod, b June 2, 1766.

Sarah, b Nov. 21, 1763.
Dorothy, b Dec. 21, 17[illegible].
3 Joshua, b Nov. 4, 1774.
4 Josiah, b Feb. 17, 177[illegible].
Olinda, b June 8, 17[illegible].

23241 ABEL, b at Lebanon June 6, 1758, enlisted as a privateer in the ship Oliver Cromwell Dec., 1777.

23242 ICHABOD, b at Lebanon June 2, 1756.

23243 JOSHUA, b Nov. 4, 1774, at Lebanon, m Lucretia Gott; moved to Wooster, Otsego County, N. Y., in 1797, and to Jefferson, Ashtabula County, O., in 1811, where he was ordained pastor of the Baptist Church and preached one year. He then removed to Sharon, Pa., where he preached for four years, after which he settled in New Lyme, Ashtabula Co., O., where he continued to reside until his death, Nov. 9, 1869. Children—
1 Story.
Sally, m Thomas Groves.
Polly, m Nelson Martin, farmer, Rome, Ash. Co., O.
Betsey.
2 William.
3 Joshua.
4 John.
5 Abel.

232431 STORY, m Candice Jayne, farmer, lives in Wisconsin.

232432 WILLIAM, farmer, Pierpont, Ashtabula Co., O., m Katherine Dickinson.

232433 JOSHUA, lives at Bangor, LaCrosse Co., Wis., m Gertrude Cortelean.

232434 JOHN, farmer, Orwell, Ashtabula Co., O., m Esther Vells. Children—
1 William N.
2 Charles H.
Betsey L., m H. B. Olmstead, has four children.
Maria E., m H. Warren, Sturges, Mich.
John W., d soon.
Helen A., m G. M. Woodworth, Cork, Ashtabula Co., O.
3 George A.
Mary J., m G. Markell, Ashtabula Co., O.
4 Rollin A.

2324341 WILLIAM N., farmer, Northfield, Rice Co., Minn., m Lucy Grant. Children—

1 Clarence R.
2 Frank W.
Emma A.
Hattie J.
Lulu.
Lois.
Clara E.

2324342 CHARLES R., farmer, went to Northfield, Minn., in 1854. He writes that the traditions of his family are that the Woodworths are of Scotch descent.

2324343 GEORGE A., farmer, Orwell, Ash Co., O. Children—
Emma.
Grace.

2324344 ROLLIN A., merchant, Woonsocket, R. I., single in 1876.

232435 ABEL, farmer, New Lyme, Ash. Co., O., m Phebe Becket.

23244 JOSIAH, b Lebanon, Ct., Feb. 17, 1777.

233 EBENEZER, b March 12, 1691, m Rebecca Smalley Dec. 27, 1717 at Lebanon, Ct. His children b at Lebanon are the following:
1 Ebenezer, b Sept. 26, 1718.
Zeruiah, b Nov. 14, 1720.
2 Eliphalet, b Sept. 24, 1722.
3 Joseph, b Oct. 19, 1724.
4 Amasa, b April 4, 1727.
Rebecca, b July 25, 1729.
5 John, b Jan. 24, 1735.
Phebe, b Aug. 9, 1737.

I quote from the Porter geneology another account of the ancestry of Ebenezer:

George Woodworth, of Ipswich, England, came on the ship Elizabeth, with his wife, Mary, to Watertown, Mass., in 1641. He died in 1676.

His son, John, was born March, 1649, and married in 1673 Rebecca Robbins, b 1647; John d Nov. 3, 1732, and Rebecca d 1676.

John's son, Ebenezer, was b March 12, 1691, and m Dec. 27, 1717, Rebecca Smalley.

I am at a loss to know on what authority this pedigree is founded. I know of no WOODWORTH settling at Watertown. There was, however, a WOODWARD who came there from England, and is the ancestor of an entirely different family, some of

whom [illegible] in Lebanon, where they were known as WOODWARDS. But Ebenezer appears with [illegible] the consensus of the Lebanon records to have been the son of Benjamin Woodworth (23).

2331 EBENEZER, b Sept. 26, 1718, at Lebanon, m Hopestill Tygert Sept. [illegible] 1742. The first four of their children were born at Lebanon, the rest probably in New Hampshire, whither EBENEZER had moved about 1760. Children—

Phebe, b July 31, 1743.
1 John, b Jan. 31, 1746.
2 Sylvanus, b Jan. 2, 1748.
3 Elijah, b Oct. 11, 1749.
Lydia, b 1751, m March 1, 1773, Increase Porter, d May 11, 1792.
4 Ezra, b 1763.
5 Ebenezer.
6 Jabez.
Dore.

23311 JOHN, b Lebanon, Ct., Jan. 31, 1746, moved early in life to Dorchester, N. H., where he with his brothers had bought a tract of land containing 800 acres. Mrs. George H. Woodworth, of Hebron, N. H., gives the following account of him: "He was a small bare-lipped man, very active in the church and exemplary in life. He was the first Town Clerk of Dorchester and he held that office for many years. In 1822 he moved with his children to Ashtabula Co., O. When he was ninety years old he was visited by one of his old friends from Dorchester, whom he entertained by felling a large tree in the woods, that the friend might report to his old neighbors what a sturdy man he still was. He married Sarah Ingraham, whose family lay claim to the township of Leeds, England, worth thousands of fortunes." JOHN d 1840. Children—
1 John, b June 23, 1776.
2 Zebina.
3 Daniel.
Sally.
4 Amasa.
5 Sylvanus.

233111 JOHN, b at Dorchester, N. H., June 23, 1776, farmer and millwright, m Chloe Bridgman March 11, 1810; moved to St. Albans, Vt., and in 1829 to Cherry Valley, Ash. Co., O. He served in the war of 1812, and d in 1858. Children—
1 Hiram.

2 Heman.

Hannah L. C., m. [illegible] Lev. Woodworth.

Mary P., m Rev. E. D. Lewis.

3 John Calvin, lawyer, d unmarried at age of 25.

4 Nathan Ingraham.

5 Horace Gideon.

233111 HIRAM, b at St. Alban, Vt., m for his first wife Lucy Smith, and for his second wife Betsy M. Higby, residence 407 19th street, Buffalo, N. Y., carpenter. Children-

Belle L.

1 Claudius Hiram.

L. Emma, m Chas. S. Webb, 373 Maryland street, Buffalo, N. Y.

2 Jesse Higby.

Minnie S.

2331111 CLAUDIUS HIRAM, insurance, 62 Main street, Buffalo, m Julia A. Schecker. Children—

Frances E.

2331112 HEMAN, carpenter, Clearwater, Mich., m Betsey Tourgee, afterwards Louisa Richmond. Children—

1 Thaddeus J.

2 D. Henry.

3 Edward Lewis.

Mary Eliza, m Henry Crowell, Minneapolis, Minn.

Susan Cordelia, m Walter Jordan, Petowka, Ill.

4 John Franklin.

Emma Evangeline.

Ella Ernestine.

5 Charles M.

23311121 THADDEUS J., Clearwater, Mich., served in the war for the Union, m Juliette Tracy Bentley. Children—

1 Earnest Edward.

2 Charles Newton.

3 George Leland.

Louisa Etta.

4 Lyle Arthur.

23311122 D. HENRY, Waseca, Minn., served in the Civil War, m Ella Thompson. Child—

Ella Elizabeth.

23311123 EDWARD LEWIS, m Isadore Carey at Minneapolis, Minn., served in the Union Army. Children—

1 Thurston.
Mabel.

2331124 JOHN FRANKLIN.

2331125 CHARLES M., d. in the war for the Union, unmarried.

2331114 NATHAN INGRAHAM, m. Jerusha Bidwell of Painesville, O., was Chaplain of the 21st Regular Infantry, Wis. Volunteers in the Civil War, is now a Baptist minister at Welaka, Fla.

2331115 HORACE GIDEON, m. Frances Jurney, of Fayette Co., Ill., is a Baptist minister at Hudson, Mich. Was Chaplain of the 47th Illinois Volunteers in the late war. Children—

Mary Cecilia, m. Loring B. Sanford, druggist, Prairie City, Ill.
1 Hale Horace.
2 Edson Snow.
3 Lee Howard, d.
Jennie and Nellie, d.
4 John Jurney, d.
5 James Grant.
6 Benjamin Holland.
7 Walter Scott.
8 Richard Paul.

Rev. Horace Gideon writes thus gayly: "As you are aware, the Woodworths against the world for doing practical works. I do not now think of any earthly prestige worth the mention. Some of the family have been talked of for Congress, never, I believe, for the penitentiary. No doubt we are a marked sprig of the genus homo, and when honest men come in fashion, we shall make a tally. There is one curious thing—you may have noticed the same—all have the same voice. I can tell a Woodworth blindfolded or in the dark, if he will speak."

23312 SYLVANUS, b. at Lebanon, Ct., Jan. 2, 1748, fought in the battle of Bunker Hill in Capt. Jas. Clark's Co., of Connecticut. The position of this company was on the extreme left, extending towards Mystic River. They were behind breastworks made of hay between two rail fences. Sylvanus accompanied President Wheelock, the founder of Dartmouth College, who then had a school at Lebanon, on his first visit to Hanover, N. H., and in 1770 he erected the first building used by the college. He was one of the original proprietors of Dorchester, Grafton County, N. H., where he and his brother had

bought a large tract of land. He was noted in that region as a bear hunter. He was a fine singer and taught a singing school during the long Winter evenings. In early life he was engaged to Tamesin Thorn, whom he devotedly loved, and whose early death he deeply mourned for many years prior to his marriage to Tamesin Nevins in 1792. He was possessed of a strong religious nature. His life was one of hardship not unmingled with adventure and romance. He died suddenly at night in the highway alone, on his way to his home, in 1797. Children—

1 George, b 1795.
2 Henry, b 1797.
3 Calvin, b 1798.

GEORGE, b 1795, at Dorchester, N. H., farmer, m Lois Hovey, b 1795. He was a school teacher in his younger days and an accomplished musician "He was a man of many virtues, universally respected, contending frequently with adversity, but never compromising a character of unblemished integrity and conscientious adherence to correct principles. He was an officer of the church and for many years a justice of the peace." I annex the following from the widow of George:

Lynn, Mass., March 17, 1876.

With pleasure I comply with Mr. Woodworth's request and give such information as I am able. I think Sylvanus Woodworth's father's name was Sylvanus, of this I am not sure; but he married Tamesin Thorn as I have heard my husband's mother say, whose name was Tamesin Nevins before she married. S. W. came up to Hanover as a laborer in the company, when Dartmouth College was moved up from Connecticut by President Wheelock. After working there awhile he went to Dorchester, some twenty miles back from Connecticut River. He bought three hundred acres of land and moved up from Connecticut with four brothers; I know not which was oldest or youngest, but their names were John, Ebenezer, Jabez and Ezra. The two latter moved to Essex County in a few years, after which time I knew little of him. John was a small hare-lipped man, who was very active in the church and exemplary in life. He was an elegant writer and was Town Clerk for a good number of years, his writing being first in the records. He moved all his children to Ashtabula Co., Ohio, after he had advanced in years. I think he was ninety years or nearly that when one of his Dorchester neighbors called to see him. He asked him to go out in the woods when he felled a tree in his presence so the

feat might be repeated in his old neighborhood. Ebenezer died of [illegible] spotted fever in Dorchester, but his widow and children accompanied uncle John with ox carts, driving cows and journeying twenty miles per day and resting Sunday. John Woodworth married Sarah Bingham of the family, who a few years ago sent an agent to England to prove their claim to the township of Leeds. I have not learned that it was a success.

Sylvanus Woodworth was in the Bunker Hill fight in Capt. Clark's company under Gen. Putnam. They made a forced march and got warm. When they came to water as many as drinked while so heated, were immediately sick. Woodworth immersed his hands above the pulse in his wrists; bathed his temples and rinsed his mouth several times before he swallowed any; then drank a little at a time until he was satisfied with drink, and received no injury from it. He taught singing and was said to have a voice that charmed. Married at 53 years and died at 57 in December, 1796.

Very truly yours,

MRS. L. H. WOODWORTH.

They had the following children:

1 Irenaeus Clinton, d.
2 William H.
   Esther T. B., m Benj. F. Ellis, merchant, Peoria, Ill.
3 Albert Bingham.
4 Edward Baker.
5 Artemus B., b 1841.
   Elizabeth K., m Peter Whittemore, farmer, Plymouth, N. H.
   Grace L., m Daniel Clement, farmer, Warren, N. H.
   Louisa M., m Lucius A. Young, druggist, Tilton, N. H.
   Sarah F., Concord, N. H.
6 George Thornton, b 183[illegible], d 1860, single, at Pewamo, Mich.
7 John Ball, d 1863, single, at Hebron, N. H.

2331212 WILLIAM HENRY, farmer and lumberman, b at Hebron, N. H. Moved when fourteen years old to Pewamo, Ionia County, Mich. Was Probate Judge for the county for a number of years. Married Caroline Matilda Balch. Children—

1 Henry Dodge.
   Bertha.

2331212 1 HENRY DODGE, b at Pewamo, Mich., m Maggie H. Rosekrans.

2331213 ALBERT BINGHAM, b at Hebron N. H., m Mary Angeline Parker; is a wholesale flour, grain and grocery merchant in Concord, N. H.

To whose kindly letters received from ALBERT, and especially from his wife, I am indebted for much interesting information regarding the family. Child—

1 Edward Knowlton.

2331214 EDWARD BAKER m Helen Maria Whiton, of Franklin, Co., Sept. 9, 1875.

2331215 ARTEMUS BROOKS b 1841, at Hebron, N. H., m Lucia Brooks. Is a lumber manufacturer at Lowell, Mass. Much of the material used in this genealogy is derived from the interesting letters of Artemas, who regards it as honor enough for the family to possess the inventor of the cylinder planing machine, and the author of the "Old Oaken Bucket." Children—

1 Artemus Brooks, Jr.

2 Henry Phelps.

Lizzie.

23312151 ARTEMUS BROOKS, JR.

233122 HENRY, b at Dorchester 1797, m and had twelve children—

1 Thomas Henry, Cincinnati.

2 Horatio Calvin, 232 State street Boston, has a son, Wilbur.

Mrs. Joseph Sanborn, Somerville, Mass. The others have not been ascertained.

233123 CALVIN, b at Dorchester 1791, m and had one son—

1 Wilbur Putnam, living at Monroe, Mich.

23313 ELIJAH, b at Lebanon Oct. 14, 1749; no further trace.

23314 EZRA, b 1763, probably at Dorchester, N. H. In his early life he removed to Essex, Chittenden Co., Vt., and in 1807 to Asutabula Co., O. He was a school teacher and an elder in the Presbyterian Church. He d at West Williamsfield, O., Jan., 1834, and his wife Anna d Aug., 1839. Children—

1 Diodate, b 1789.

2 Albigence, b 1794.

3 Horatio.

4 Luther.

5 Cyril.

[illegible] Wheaton, [illegible], Williamsfield, O.
[illegible]rlnda, m [illegible] Anderson, [illegible], Andover, O.

233141 DORANCE, b 179[illegible], [illegible] Wayne, Ash. Co., O., m Jerusha Percival; served in the war of 1812. Children—
Ann.
Emeline.
Sophia.
Juliana.
Sabra.
All m farmers living in Wayne and Williamsfield, O.
1 Cyrus.
2 Abel.
3 Richard.
4 Darius.

2331411 CYRUS, farmer, Wayne, O.

2331412. ABEL, farmer, Williamsfield, O.

2331413 RICHARD, Congregational minister, Wheatland, Mich.

2331414 DARIUS, Congregational minister, Thompson, Grange, Co., O., m Almira Snow. Has one son—
1 Lee.

23314141 LEE, m Louisa Osborn.

233142 ALBIGENCE, b 1794, farmer, Wayne, Ash. Co., O., m for first wife Margaret Whiton, and for his second, an English lady. He d 1875 Children—
1 Reuben, b 1822.
2 Albigence.
Ellen M., m Brooks, 160 State street, Chicago, Ill.
3 Newell.

2331421 REUBEN, b 1822, farmer, West Williamsfield, O., m Laura Kingsley. Children—
Josephine L., b 1855.
Orsen, d at age of ten.
Lucinda, d at age of three.
1 Leverett S., b 1846.

23314211 LEVERETT S., b 1846, Congregational minister, at Campello, Mass., graduated from Brown University in 1871; from Andover Theological Seminary in 1874, m Josephine C. Field, b 1845. Children—

1 Jesse Reuben, b 1876.

233143 HORATIO, farmer, Wayne Co., O., m Charity Ketchum. Children—
Elvira, m Luther White.
1 Calvin.
2 Horatio.
Elizabeth, m Albert Walker, farmer, Ill.
Charity, m Anson Knowles, farmer, Wayne, O.
Tryphena, m Edward Dodge, carpenter, Colebrook, O.
Florella, d.
3 Newton O.
4 Addison.
5 Cyril.

2331431 CALVIN, m Susan Smith, lives at Allen Creek, Oceana Co., Mich., carpenter.

2331432 HORATIO, farmer, m Emily Smith.

2331433 NEWTON O., m Almira Petry, d.

2331434 ADDISON, lives at Wayne, O., unmarried (1876).

2331435 CYRIL, farmer, Wayne Co., O., m Rachel M. Forbes. Children—
1 Orlandus.
Sarah Ann.
2 Joseph F.
3 Willis C.
Flora T.
Charity.

23315 EBENEZER, b probably at Dorchester, N. H., d of spotted fever. His widow and children moved with John to Ashtabula Co., O., about 1807. I have not been able to learn the names of their children or descendants.

23316 JABEZ, b about 1755, probably at Dorchester; moved with his brother Ezra to Essex, Vt., farmer, m Elizabeth Clark. Children—

1 Jabez.
2 Jonathan, b Nov. 11, 1783.
Elizabeth, m John Reynolds.
3 Ruba.
4 Asaph.
5 Ebenezer.
Hopestill, m Horace Shurvin.

[illegible]

233161 [illegible]

233162 JONATHAN, b [illegible] 1793, m Harriet Menzes, d [illegible] 17, 18[illegible], at Wooster, O. Children—

1 Henry D.
2 Jonathan.
Harriet.
Mary.

2331621 HENRY D., b Aug [illegible] 1812, [illegible] 1 [illegible] Lane. 2. Messala Ruby. He d at Kansas City, Mo., Jan. [illegible] 188[illegible]. His widow survives him. Children by first wife:

Medora, m George Whitehead, Denver, Col.
Cornelia, m. ---- [illegible], Denver, Col.

By his second wife—

1 James Ruby.
2 William H., Chicago.
3 John, d.
Mattie.
Kittie.

23316211 JAMES RUBY, m Harriet Sawyer Barrett, is a practicing lawyer at Kansas City, Mo. Children—

Mellicent Medora, b Aug. 8, 1870, at Kansas City, now a teacher in high school in Wooster, O.
Leon Aldrich, d.

233163 [illegible], b , farmer and starch manufacturer, Underhill, Vt.; was adjutant and acting general in the war of 1812, at the battle of Plattsburg. Married three times, 1 Orphelia Lane, d 18[illegible]; 2 Tellera See, d 1842; 3 Abigail Gilman. Children—

1 Nelson.
[illegible], m [illegible] Powell, farmer, Underhill, Vt.
[illegible], m [illegible], merchant, Underhill, Vt.
[illegible] M., m [illegible] Bicknell, lumber dealer, Underhill, Vt.
2 [illegible].
[illegible], d [illegible].
3 [illegible].
[illegible], m [illegible] Lyndick, Underhill, Vt.

233163[illegible] NELSON, [illegible] m Ann [illegible].

2331623 BYRON, b Underhill, Vt., m in California, d 1859.

233164 ASAPH, b , m Harriet [illegible].

233165 EBENEZER, b , m Lucy Honeywood.

233166 CLARK, b , m Adeline Rogers.

2332 ELIPHALET, b Sept. 21, 1722. According to information I have received, the accuracy of which, however, I cannot vouch for, the following are the names of his children:
1 Eliphalet, b 1751.
2 Ebenezer.
3 Joshua, b about 1760.
4 Amasa, b 1764.

23321 ELIPHALET, b at Lebanon 1751, m Priscilla , b 1753. He d Oct. 16, 1826; she d Oct. 12, 1838, and both are buried in the churchyard at Columbia, Ct., with their children—
Zeruiah, b 1781, d Jan. 18, 1810.
Sarah, b 1793, d March 18, 1796.

23323 JOSHUA, m Esther Fuller. He was a farmer and lived in South Coventry, Ct.; he served in the war of 1812.
1 Spencer, b 1780.
2 Asa.
3 Jesse.
4 Perry, b June, 1797.
Sophy, m [illegible], farmer, South Coventry.
Eunice, m John Bell, farmer, So. Coventry.
Ada, m Erastus Lincoln, shoemaker, So. Coventry.

233231 SPENCER, b at So. Coventry, Ct., 1780, m Nov. 24, 1808, Amanda Clark, b 1782, daughter of John Clark of So. Coventry. They moved to Rochester, N. Y., in 18[illegible], where he bought a farm about two miles out of the city on which he lived

[illegible] Naples [illegible] Chancellor [illegible] [illegible] B. Campbell [illegible] [illegible] 1 [illegible] 7, [illegible] [illegible] [illegible] d. 22.

1 J[illegible] S., b Sept [illegible], 1843
Sarah R., b [illegible] d [illegible] 10, 18[illegible].

2 F[illegible], b May [illegible]

3 Chauncey B[illegible], b [illegible] 2, 1841
Mark, b March 27, [illegible] d [illegible]

4 [illegible] A., b Oct. 1, 18[illegible].

5 Clark A., b April 9, 18[illegible]

233[illegible]11 JOHN SPENCER, b So. Coventry, Ct., Oct. 23, 1815, m Mary [illegible] Stanton March, 1842. JOHN S. d in Rochester, N. Y., May 9, 1[illegible] d Aug. 12, 1[illegible]. No children.

233[illegible]12 RUFUS, b So. Coventry, Ct., May 5, 1817, m Lavi[illegible] [illegible], Steuben County, N. Y., Sept. 17, 1841. He d Nov. 2[illegible], 18[illegible]

233[illegible]13 CHAUNCEY BOOTH, b So. Coventry, Ct., Feb. 2[illegible], 1819, m J[illegible] 1841 Martha J. S[illegible], b in Chelsea, Mass., Jan. 2, 1823. Chauncey is a large manufacturer of perfumery at Rochester, N. Y.; was [illegible] of Monroe Co., 18[illegible] to 18[illegible]. Children —

1 Chauncey C., b Feb. 5, 1845.
Helen A., b March 15, 1846, m Pierce C. Smith July, 1875.
Lillie J., b May 2, 1848, d Feb. 5, 1851.

2 Frank F., b Oct. 16, 18[illegible], m Anna Warren.

3 Harry S., b Aug. 16, 1856, m Mary Stevens.

2332[illegible]131 CHAUNCEY C., b at Rochester, N. Y., Feb. 5, 18[illegible], [illegible] from Williams College in 186[illegible]; was a member of the firm of [illegible] B. Woodworth & Sons manufacturers of perfumery [illegible] 18[illegible] [illegible] 18[illegible]; was a member of the Executive Board of the city of Rochester and in charge of the Water, Fire and Highway Departments from 1876 to 18[illegible]; was Secretary of the Rochester City & Brighton R. R. Co. from 18[illegible] to [illegible] [illegible] City National Bank of Rochester [illegible] 18[illegible], and [illegible] Rochester Trust & Safe Deposit Co., [illegible] since 18[illegible]. [illegible] Susan Elizabeth Merrell, Sept. [illegible] [illegible] John [illegible] [illegible] at Rochester, April [illegible] 18[illegible]. Her [illegible] Elizabeth [illegible] [illegible] at New England [illegible] 18[illegible] [illegible]

1 Edward [illegible], b Dec. 21, 18[illegible].

2 Chauncey [illegible], b Sept. 23, 18[illegible], d [illegible] 18[illegible]

Maria [illegible] 1847.
[illegible] 25, 18[illegible].
[illegible]

The following is an extract from a letter written by Oliver Woodworth, of New [illegible] to Chauncey C. Woodworth of Rochester, dated April 2[illegible], 18[illegible].

"The name of your ancestor Joshua, I do not remember to have ever heard mentioned by my parents or uncles. But it seems somewhat singular that my father [illegible] with his family to the same Coventry you speak of about [illegible] and lived there nine years. I have a sister with me who was born in Coventry and moved from there in 1817 to Vermont, and who remembers many things about the place but no one of the same name. If any connection can be traced it must go back to my father's uncles, but he was very careful to speak of all cousins, and never having heard him mention one of that name leads me to suppose there is no connection that can be traced. We have no old family records and I have never been able to find and trace back beyond my grandfather Asa."

The following letter from Mr. C. C. Woodworth, of Rochester, to his father, dated April, 1881, is quoted at length: "Dear father: I left Springfield Friday morning at seven and changed cars at Palmer for So. Coventry. It is a very old fashioned place, scattered over a mile or more along the valley with three or four stores in the front part of a residence. Several mills have been started there in the last fifteen or eighteen years which makes up the population; but as near as I can see, everybody that can, moves away to some more lively place. I found two of our branch of the family living there, but saw only one, Albert [illegible]. Woodworth. He is a cousin of yours. He has no written family records, but says that Joshua W. Woodworth your grandfather, had four sons—Asa, Jesse, Spencer and Harry. He and his brother James are sons of Harry Woodworth, who died some years ago. Your father had two sisters, Lucy, who married a Lincoln, died some three years ago, but has a daughter living who is your cousin, and a sister who married John Eels, who was buried only last week. Asa, another brother of your father, had sons Charles, Oliver, George, Augustus and Leonard. George and Augustus live in Stafford and Andover nearly; others are dead. There are two daughters of Asa, also Laura and Maria. Of Oliver and his children he knew nothing; thinks he died early. Jesse, the other brother, had three children Martha, Waterman and Ansel. One of them (Ansel) lives somewhere in New York State—Waterman at Broadbrook, 16 miles

[illegible] hardly [illegible] Nov. [illegible] and [illegible] very [illegible] pages [illegible] word for his [illegible] down to 1840. I find that [illegible] Woodward, your uncle, was born June, 1795. I find that Spencer Woodworth, Shubal W[illegible], Ira Lillie and Ansel [illegible] were chosen tythingmen for the year ending Dec., 18[illegible]7. But there were Woodworths there before Joshua M., for I find it entered that Anne Woodworth, daughter of Joseph W., was born Nov. 6, 17[illegible]. I find this entry also: "Dec. ye 1726: desired by Mr. Riggs to appear [illegible] a steer coming two years old, [illegible], [illegible] ye right eare, two slits on ye fore; pricd at thirty shillings." Josiah Colburn, Ichabod Woodworth. Now, who Ichabod was, mentioned in 1726, and who Anne was in 1756, and her father, Joseph, I can't find out. There was a Simeon Woodworth there in later years —1825 to 1840— who had sons and daughters, but was no relation to the tribe of Joshua. It is a curious study and if I had had more time I might have found out more. I saw and talked with an old man who had the church register. I I find that Spencer Woodworth was collector and paid the amount on Sept. 22, 1817, of $271.52 in full. I find that William Woodworth and Mary Knox were married by Chauncey Booth Oct. 11, 1831. The man who keeps the cemetery, C. W. Jacobs, I will write to. He might find something on the gravestones.

"There are twenty or thirty Woodworths in Boston. Some of them may know of the earlier history, but the family is over two hundred years old in this country, and as they multiply it becomes more and more difficult. Joshua must have had a lot of brothers and his father likewise, and in those early days when they scattered, they never knew much about each other afterwards. I saw Charles B. Woodworth at the American Mfg. Co., Chicopee Falls, Mass., who gave me the name of his grandfather who lived in Coventry. His name was [illegible], born about 1784. He might have been a brother of Joshua M. Woodworth."

EGBERT AUGUSTUS, b. at Rochester, N. Y., Oct. 1, 18[illegible], m. Amanda Smith; lived at [illegible], Genesee Co., N. Y.; d. Jan. 3, 18[illegible].

[illegible] CLARK L., b [illegible] Rochester, N. Y., April 9, 18[illegible] m Julia Ann[illegible] B[illegible] [illegible] April 9, 18[illegible]; [illegible] at [illegible], M[illegible] Co., N. Y. Children—
1 William A[illegible], b in G[illegible], N. Y., Aug. 19, 1[illegible].
L[illegible] Beth, b [illegible], N. Y., Feb. 1[illegible], 18[illegible]3, d Jan. 16, 1868.

2[illegible]323[illegible] WILLIAM ANSEL, b in G[illegible], N. Y., Aug. 19, 18[illegible] m Eleanor W. Shipman April 2[illegible], 18[illegible]. Children—
Ethel, b A[illegible] 3, 1887.
Clark, b April 11, 1891.

23[illegible]232 ASA, m Sally Boynton, So. Coventry, Ct., farmer. Children—
1 Charles, d.
2 Oliver, d.
3 George Stafford, Ct.
4 Augustus, Andover, Mass.
5 Leonard, d.
Laura Maria.

233233 JESSE, m Myra Whittemore; farmer, So. Coventry, Ct. Children—
Martha.
1 Waterman C., Broadbrook, Ct.
2 Ansel, New York State.

233234 HARRY, b So. Coventry, Ct., June, 1797, m Roxy Robinson. Children—
1 James.
2 Lucian.
3 Henry.
4 Albert Payne.
Olive, m Ezra Gross, farmer, Willimantic, Ct.
Miranda, m A. Gladding, farmer, So. Coventry.
Eliza, m Ashbel Roberts, farmer, Mansfield, Ct.
Harriet, single.

2332341 JAMES, m Julia Roberts, farmer, So. Coventry.

2332342 LUCIAN, m Mary McCracken, farmer, Mansfield, Ct.; served in the war of the Union.

2332343 HENRY, m Amerett Crossman, farmer, Mansfield, Ct.; served in the war for the Union.

2332344 ALBERT PAYNE, m Ellen A. Austin, carpenter, So. Coventry; served in the war for the Union. Children—
Olive B.
1 Arthur L.
2 Therçon P.

3 Wesley [illegible].

Ida May.

2373 JOSEPH, b Oct. 15, 1725, at Lebanon, Ct., m Rebecca W[illegible], b Sep 24, 17[illegible], of Lebanon, May 12, 1748. Moved to Nova Scotia in 17[illegible] with his brother, [illegible], and settled at Horton, where he d March 29, 179[illegible]; his wife d May 14, 18[illegible]6. Children—

1 Samuel, b Lebanon, April 11, 1748.

Annie, b Coventry, Ct., Nov. 6th, 1756.

Joseph, b Lebanon, June 23, 1759, d Oct. 19, 1761, at Horton, N. S.

2 Joseph, b Horton, N. S., April 15, 1761.

James, b Horton, N. S., 1768, d 1769.

3 Elihu, b Horton, N. S., May 17, 1771.

(The foregoing account beginning on page 40 contains a number of errors and omissions, an opportunity for the correction of which, from information received since the foregoing was put in print, occurs at this point:

23322 JOSHUA, b about 1760, m Esther Fuller Aug. 23, 1778. He appears, by the New London records to have owned lands there in 1770. His daughter, Ada, is incorrectly said on page 40, to have married Erastus Lincoln. She married Hazard Tinker, and her sister, Lucy Clark, m Erastus Lincoln. Joshua had also a son Elias, bap. 1792.

Page 41, first line, SPENCER, d Nov. 7, 1855; his wife d July 8, 1861, his daughter, Lucy, was m Feb. 22, 1837.

233231 JOHN SPENCER, m Mary L. Williams.

2332213 CHAUNCEY B.'s daughter, Lillie J., d Feb. 6, 1854; his son, Frank E., m Oct. 14, 1879.

2332213 CHAUNCEY C.'s wife's mother's name was Ann Maria Smith.

On page 42, ALBERT C. WOODWORTH should read ALBERT P. WOODWORTH.

2332311 EGBERT AUGUSTUS, b at Rochester, N. Y., Oct. 1, 1823, m Sept. 7, 1845, Amanda M. Smith, who was b at Chelsea, Mass., March 23, 1824, and d at Rochester Aug. 3, 1889. They lived at Linden, Genesee Co., N. Y. Egbert d Jan. 3, 1885. Children—

Frances Amanda, b Aug. 10, 1846.

1 George Egbert, b June 29, 1848, d Sept. 11, 1849.

2 Harry Livingston, b Sept. 4, 1850, d Oct. 19, 1873.

3 Wm. Walker, b July 31, 1853.

Cora Eugenia, b Feb. 7, 1856, d June 19, 1858.

4 Samuel Hea[illegible] b Aug. 13, 1[illegible].
  Mintie Bell, b March 11, 18[illegible], d March 21, 1[illegible]61.
5 Charles [illegible], b June 12, 18[illegible].
  Ruby Estelle, b Feb. 1, 18[illegible].

On page 4[illegible], the following corrections should be made:

232232 ASA, bap. Oct. 17[illegible], m Sally B[illegible]ington, Nov. 30, 180[illegible].

232233 JESSE, bap. Oct., 17[illegible], m, first, Lucy Fuller; had children—
  Tryphena.
  Martha Waterman.
  Ansel.

232234 HARRY was b June 23, 1797, and d 1873.

23331 SAMUEL, b Lebanon, April 11, 17[illegible]8, m Levina ——; had two sons b at Hebron, Ct.—
1 Samuel, b Oct. 5, 1795.
2 Asahel, b Dec. 1, 1797.

23332 JOSEPH, b Horton, N. S., April 15, 1764, m possibly Charlotte Cleveland. The only child of which I have any information is—
1 Joseph, b Grand Pre, N. S., Dec. 29, 1795.

233321 JOSEPH, b Grand Pre, N. S., Dec. 29, 1795, m Charlotte Neary, 1821, d Dec. 16, 1841. Children—
1 James Elihu, b Nov. 1, 1822.
2 John Clark, b May 10, 1824.
3 Leander, b Jan. 13, 1827, d Sept. 20, 1846.
  Harriet A., b April 7, 1827, m 1850.
4 Charles Henry, b Feb. 16, 1830.
5 Edwin, b July 20, 1831, d Nov. 7, 1846.
  Charlotte, b July 26, 1842, m Aug., 1854.
6 Lewis, b March 8, 1835.
  Emma L., b Sept. 3, 1836, m Jan., 1856.
  Mary Eliza, b May 10, 1833, m in Boston, Jan. 5, 1876, Lysander P. Freeman.
  Joseph, b 1841, d 1842.

2333211 JAMES ELIHU, b Wolfville, N. S., Nov. 1, 1822, m Aug. 30, 1849, Caroline Leggard, of Halifax; occupation, builder. Children—
  Ella, b Morrisania, N. Y., June 29, 1852.
  Ida D., b Wolfville, N. S., April 29, 1855.
1 Frederick William, b ——, June 26, 1857.

23332111 FREDERICK WM., b Wolfville, N. S., June 26, 1857, m at Boston, Mass., Oct. 4, 1881.

2333212 JOHN CLARK, b Wolfville, N. S., May 10, 1824, m 1855.

2333213 [illegible], b Wolfville, Jan. 13, 1827, d Sept. 29, [illegible]

2333211 CHARLES HENRY, b Wolfville Feb. 16, 1829, m and lives in Boston.

2333216 LEWIS, b Wolfville, March 8, 1835, m in Boston, July 4, 1856, d Wolfville, 1858.

23333 ELIHU, b Horton, N. S., May 17, 1771, m Sabre Davidson March 3, 1793, d July 7, 18[illegible]. Children—

Clarissa, b March 20, 1794, d May 5, 1828, single.
1 Samuel, b March 13, 1798.
Anna, b May 16, 1801, m James Pellmeter 1824, d June 23, 1827.
2 Benjamin, b July 28, 1803.
Sarah, b Sept. 5, 1806, m E. W. Dawson, 1832, d June 8, 1855, leaving one son—J. B. Dawson, real estate and insurance, Wolfville, N. S.
Eunice Rebecca, b March 13, 1810, d March 21, 1845.
Mary Alice, b Aug. 9, 1813, m John Duncan, St. John, N. B.
3 John W., b Nov. 5, 1816.

233331 SAMUEL, b March 13, 1798, m, had no children, d March 11, 1882; his wife d May 10, 1882.

233332 BENJAMIN, b July 28, 1803, m Charlotte Ellis. Children—
1 Elihu.
Sabra, m Capt. Theodore Harris.
2 John A.
Two other children deceased.

2333321 ELIHU, lives at Sackville, N. B., journalist.

2333322 JOHN A., lives at Grand Pre, N. S.

The following letter received from John A. by George W. (2321212) contains an interesting account of the Nova Scotia branch of the family:

Grand Pre, N. S., Nov. 8th, 1880.

George W. Woodworth, Esq., St. Louis, Mo.:

Dear Sir. Some time since I received a letter from you asking for information of the Woodworth family. I have to apologize for not having answered it more promptly, and can only plead press of business at the time of the receipt of it and it slipped from my memory since. I should probably have been more prompt if I had had anything to send you more than you already possess, as my brother, E. W., of Kentville, enclosed me a similar letter to the one you sent me some time before, and I understood from him that he

[illegible] sent you a copy [illegible] the only [illegible] family [illegible] Woodworth [illegible] New England branching [illegible] to Grand Pré (Horton) about the year 1760 or '61. The townships of Horton and Cornwallis were settled about that time to two hundred families from New England, chiefly from Connecticut and Massachusetts, and a few from Rhode Island, and took of the [illegible] and took possession of the rich dyked lands reclaimed from the sea by the French Acadians who were expelled some twelve years before. At that time came two, if not three, families of Woodworths, not claiming any kinship, although I have been told by some of the older ones that the tradition was that only two brothers of the name came to New England and from them spring the families claiming American descent. These were New England Loyalists of the name settled on the St. John River in New Brunswick. All of the Woodworths I have ever heard of, with but one exception, were descended from the New England families; the exception is a policeman in Fredericton, N. B., and he was formerly an English soldier. I am probably writing you about what you are much better acquainted with than I and what would be of little use to you in the work you have undertaken and in which I wish you every success. If I can be of any service to you I should be most happy. If I knew to whom you have written in Nova Scotia and New Brunswick, I would know better then if I could be of any assistance; also if you want a record of all families to date. Perhaps a few words about the families I know something about might be interesting to you, if not useful. There seem to be points of resemblance in the families here that would warrant the supposition of having sprung from a common ancestry; for instance, they are mostly a large race of men, not extraordinary, but well grown, from five feet ten to six feet. Not seeking after notoriety and undemonstrative enough to have descended from one of Cromwell's Ironsides. There has always been for the last hundred years one of the name land surveyor; most of the name have been farmers, with a few mechanics, and not a few in the learned professions. One lawyer, a politician, Douglas B. or "Doug," has given the name a greater notoriety throughout Canada than it has had since Samuel, of Scituate, wrote the "Old Oaken Bucket." He is at present in Manitoba, where he is a candidate for the local house, he having been beaten in this, his own county, last election. His brother, George W. Woodworth, a namesake of your own, runs a local paper in Kentville. This is a different branch of the family from ours, although the same given names are common—Benjamin and Joseph, Rebecca, Sarah and Mary, etc. I think it

233333 JOHN WM., b Nov. 5, 1816, m Jane Caldwell June 11, 1[illegible] d July 24, 1846.

2334 AMASA, b Lebanon, Ct., April 4, 1727; went to Nova Scotia in 1765 with his brother, Joseph, and bought lands in Cornwallis. He afterwards returned to Connecticut and then moved to Vermont, after which I find no trace of him, except that he m Sarah ——, and had one child—

Israel, d June 8, 1769, at Cornwallis, aged 1½ years.

2335 JOHN, b Lebanon, Ct., Jan. 24, 1735.

234 AMOS, m Ellie Mathews Oct. 3, 1723. Both are mentioned in Richard Newcomb's store book, 1735 to 1738 and his name also appears in a rate bill of Columbia Church, in 1741.

235 EZEKIEL, mentioned in the Lebanon records as one of the petitioners for a new church at Lebanon Crank. In 1723 he is the grantee of land from his father, Benjamin. In 17[illegible] he is grantor of land to his brother, Ichabod. His name appears on Richard Newcomb's store book. He is mentioned in a rate bill of Columbia Church in 1741. He may be the Ezekiel who married Lydia Stanmeta, Nov. 11 1723.

236 CALEB, probably baptized in 1704 as the name then appears on the church records of Lebanon; is mentioned in Newcomb's store book 1735 to 1738; is grantee of land from his brother, Ebenezer, in 1735. After 1738 there is no trace of Caleb in Lebanon during his life. He probably moved with his sister, Judith, wife of Thomas Newcomb, to Salisbury, Ct., for in the town records there appears in 1749 a deed from Thomas Newcomb to Caleb Woodworth of 1[illegible] acres of land "of a division to be laid out hereafter." In 17[illegible] he was appointed surveyor of roads at Salisbury. In 1761 there appears a certificate to the effect that Caleb attended the Baptist [illegible]

[illegible] to [illegible] [illegible] was born in Salisbury—

1 Caleb.
2 Cyr[illegible]us.
3 S[illegible], at Salisbury May [illegible], 17[illegible].

(For further account [illegible] page [illegible].)

From the probate records [illegible] Norwich, it [illegible] that [illegible] in 1779 [illegible] estate of £7[illegible], which was divided [illegible] his widow, (whose name is [illegible]) and his heirs, [illegible] children, as follows.

[illegible] 1 Asa, 3d, b 1744.
Sarah.
Ruth.
Hannah.
2 Simeon.
3 Jasper.
4 Charles.
5 Amos.
Eunice, m Mr. Inglis Nov. 20, 1786; admitted to old Norwich Church, 1822.

2301 ASA, b 1744, known as Asa 3d. He m Elizabeth Kingsley July 25, 1767, and with his wife was admitted to the old Norwich Church by letter in 1772. He died Feb. 22, 1813, and was buried in the old church yard at Norwich Town, by the side of his son, Dyer. He left a will dated June 30, 1812, in which he mentions his wife Elizabeth and his children, Enos, Eunice, Asa and Hannah. The other Asas in the neighborhood and mentioned in this record as 522 and [illegible]. Children were:

1 Dyer, b Oct. 16, 1768, d June 2, 1783.
2 Enos, bap. April 20, 1771
3 Asa, bap. Sept. 8, 177[illegible].
4 [illegible], bap. May 12, 1776, d young.
Eunice, bap. Oct. 31, 1772, d 18[illegible].
Hannah, bap. July [illegible], 1785.
Elizabeth, widow of ASA, d 1835, aged 92.

2[illegible] JASPER. There is a grave stone in Columbia burying ground in memory of Jasper, who d Sep. 6, 1811. He m Polly Lathrop and had one son, Charles [illegible] at [illegible] a carpenter, who moved West.

George H. We[illegible] of [illegible] N. Y. [illegible] JASPER, of [illegible], who [illegible] [illegible] I had [illegible] only [illegible] Jasper in the records of Norwich and vicinity and it is therefore quite possible that JASPER [illegible] the ancestor of the following family:

2363 CALEB, son of Jasper [illegible] Freeman, March 12, 17[illegible]. He was a cobbler and lived in Norwich, Ct. Children:
Harriet, b May 30, 1[illegible] Crew, d April 1[illegible], 1[illegible]9.
[illegible] Nov. 1[illegible], 1[illegible], d Sept. 22, [illegible]
[illegible], b Aug. [illegible] m [illegible] Andrews, d May 9, 1[illegible]
1 Henry Dudley, b March 2, 1[illegible]7.
2 Hezekiah Freeman, b March 16, 1811, d 18[illegible].
Martha Freeman, b April 19, 1813, d Dec. 21, 1815.
3 John W. Fletcher, b Dec. 24, 1815, d Nov. 17, 1855.

236311 HENRY DUDLEY, b at Norwich, March 2, 1807, m (1) Elizabeth L. Suydam March 15, 1832, she d Aug. 25, 1870, m (2) Sarah [illegible] Vanderbilt, Dec. 25, 1871, she d Nov. 30, 1889; he d Sept. 30, 188[illegible]. He was a teacher. Children:
1 Jacob Suydam.
Sarah Elizabeth, b Feb. 25, 1856.
2 George Henry, b March 22, 1858.

2363111 JACOB SUYDAM, m Mary Lyons in 1[illegible]; he was a teacher; lived at 268 Ryerson street, Brooklyn, d July 10, 188[illegible]. Only child:
Helen Suydam, d March 2[illegible], 1889.

2363112 GEORGE HENRY, b March 22, 1858, m Sept. 25, 1890, Charlotte Amelia Van Pelt. He is a real estate agent at 1,068 Gates avenue, Brooklyn; his residence is 731 Jefferson avenue, Brooklyn. Children:
1 George Henry, Jr., b July 7, 1891.
Helen Dudley, b June 11, 1893.

2364 CHARLES, a Revolutionary soldier from Connecticut, 177[illegible].

2365 AMOS. This may be the ancestor of the following family but I have no certain information about it; [illegible] from a [illegible] of facts and coincidences I am led to infer that Amos, son of Caleb, and Amos, father of Uriah and others are the same person. AMOS, b in Connecticut, probably prior to 17[illegible], [illegible] Newfield. AMOS was a Revolutionary soldier. He was by trade a [illegible] He moved early in life to [illegible], N. Y., and [illegible] to [illegible], Oneida County, N. Y. He had a large family of chil-

2 Wilson.
3 Reid.
4 Caleb.
5 Asa.
6 Amos.
  Katherine.
  Silas.
  Eunice.
7 David.
Katherine, Eunice, Asa and Caleb settled in Ohio, the rest in New York State.

23652 WILLIAM.

23656 AMOS, b at Stillwater, N. Y., m Matilda Rice, of Tynmouth, Vt. AMOS was a farmer and lived most of his life at Florence, N. Y., served in the War of 1812; held the offices of Justice of the Peace and Supervisor many years; served two terms as side judge in Oneida County Court; was in 1825 elected to the Assembly. He died at Sterling, Cayuga Co., N. Y., aged 63 years. Children—

  Eunice C., m Jonathan W. File, farmer and wagon maker, Chicago.
1 James Barnes, m Minerva Wiggins, farmer.
  Mary Ann, m Randall Barnes, Jefferson Co., N. Y.
  Sarah Ann, m Don. C. Wiggins, Auburn, N. Y.
  Persis S., m Elias Hardy, farmer, Auburn, N. Y.
2 Samuel S., farmer, m Cordelia Steel, afterwards Cynanthe Bushnell; lived at Owasca Co.
3 Henry A., m Emily Brown, farmer, Serlba, Oswego Co.
4 Harvey Rice.

236561 HARVEY RICE, b at Florence, Oneida County, N. Y., m Esther Ann Lawton, farmer; lives at Volney, Oswego Co. Children—

1 Gary Eddy, m Caroline E. Wales, has one son.
  Florence Eliza.
2 Amos Lawton.

24 ISAAC, b Little Compton, R. I., 1675. He may have moved to Lebanon, for in the Clerk's office at Lebanon there is a record of a

[illegible]
[illegible]
1 David [illegible]
Grace [illegible]

[illegible] DAVID, [illegible] 1697, [illegible] Nov. [illegible] He [illegible] have [illegible] the [illegible] I have [illegible] of Isaac of Norwich [illegible] Walter, Sr., [illegible] the [illegible] David of Norwich was the son of Isaac of Norwich.

[illegible] THOMAS, b at Little Compton, R. I., [illegible] Children—
Hannah, b March 5, [illegible]
Hannah, b March 5, 1772.
Lydia, b Oct. 11, [illegible]
Rachel, b March 27, [illegible]
1 Thomas, b Aug. 11, [illegible]

---

3 THOMAS, son of Walter, Sr., of Scituate, was appointed by the Court in [illegible] "to tend the wolf traps and baite them, the town to allow [illegible] for the yeare, besides pay for the wolves [illegible]" He was appointed Clerk of the Market in [illegible] and held the office till 1711. In 1712 he was made Sealer of Weights and Measures. He kept a [illegible] shop [illegible] rods south of Stockbridge's Mill. In 16[illegible]6 Scituate was sacked and plundered by the Narragansett Indians under Canonchet, and many of its houses were burned, among which was the home of THOMAS. His loss was £40. Dean says that THOMAS bought lands in Little Compton, R. I., in 1674, and some of his children may have moved there after the [illegible] He married Feb. 8, 16[illegible], Deborah Pardon. Children—

Deborah, b Jan. 2, 1667, d 1710, left will probated March, [illegible]
1 Hezekiah, b Feb. [illegible], so say Scituate records, [illegible]
Katherine, b Oct. 5, [illegible], so say Scituate records.
Ebenezer, b May 25, 1673, d young.
Mary, b July [illegible], m. Stephen [illegible], Jr.
2 John, b Aug. [illegible], Scituate records.
Hannah, b Sept. 7, 1685, Scituate records.
Jerusha, b Dec. [illegible], 1688, Scituate records.
3 Ebenezer, b Aug. [illegible], Scituate records.

21 HEZEKIAH, b Feb. [illegible] The [illegible] Dean says he married Hannah [illegible] but for reasons heretofore stated, it is probable that the Hezekiah who married Hannah [illegible]

[illegible] Benjamin [illegible] He[illegible] married Lydia [illegible] of Scituate, [illegible] of Walter [illegible] Hezekiah [illegible] son of Benjamin 22, but [illegible] are circumstances [illegible] Deane's statement [illegible] also Ezekiel, whoever he was, had a son, Benjamin, who moved to Nova Scotia, is confirmed by the report received from [illegible] Nova Scotia families who trace their descent from Ezekiel. That [illegible] had a brother Benjamin, father of Peleg, and ancestor of a large family in the United States, seems to be established by the testimony of many members of that family. Mr. James S. Woodworth of Worcester, Mass., writes that his ancestor, Benjamin, "with his brother Ezekiel" settled in Lebanon about 17[illegible], and that Ezekiel's son Benjamin "went to Nova Scotia." Other letters corroborate this statement. Ezekiel and Benjamin, therefore, were brothers. But Benjamin, the brother of Ezekiel [illegible], is the ancestor of another family and could not be the father of Peleg, because Peleg was born Oct. 21, 1720, and by reference to the family of Benjamin (22) it would have been a physical impossibility for him to have come in between Benjamin, b June 8, 1722, and Desire, b Jan. 10, 172[illegible]. The brothers therefore belonged to a different family from Benjamin (22) and there is good reason for believing Deane's statement that Ezekiel was the son of Hezekiah and on the testimony of Jas. S. Woodworth and others we must give to Ezekiel a brother, Benjamin, and, therefore, to Hezekiah a son, Benjamin. Thus the Benjamin branch is supplied with an ancestor which would not be possible if Ezekiel were taken to be the son of Benjamin 22. While this disposition of the family is not entirely satisfactory it has at least the merit of tallying better than any other with known facts. Children—

1 Ezekiel.
2 Benjamin.

311 EZEKIEL, m Lydia Simmons, of Scituate, Nov. 11, 1725. (See Deane's History of Scituate.) The only child I have discovered is:

1 Benjamin, b May 31, 1730.

And perhaps William and Thomas.

3111 BENJAMIN, b May 31, 1730 in Connecticut, m Hannah Hill; moved to Cornwallis, N. S., about 1760. His name occurs among the original grantees of land from King George, d July [illegible] 17[illegible]. Children—

1 Shelomith, b March 5, 17[illegible].
2 Benjamin.

[illegible] [illegible] N. S. [illegible] the [illegible] of [illegible] May [illegible] N. S. [illegible]

Hannah, b Nov. 28, [illegible] N. S.

John, b [illegible] 18, [illegible] St. Andrews, N. S.

1 Benjamin, b Feb. [illegible]

Lydia, b Jan. 11, 1[illegible] Knowles [illegible], Lower Stewiacke, N. S.

Sarah, b Nov. 25, [illegible] Absalom Pickings, [illegible]

2 Ingraham W., b Feb. 9, 1807.

3 Azael, b May 22, 1[illegible]9.

Nancy, b May 30, 1811, m Wm. Faulkner, surveyor, Truro, N. S.

311111 BENJAMIN, b Lower Stewiacke, N. S., Feb. 5, 1[illegible]01, farmer, m Jane F. O'Brien.

311112 INGRAHAM WILLIAM b Feb. 9, 1807, m Hannah Melton[illegible]. During his youth he was a great traveler and became a highly accomplished man. He held several important government offices. He died Feb. 9, 1863, leaving no children.

311113 AZAEL, b May 22, 1809, m Louisa Williams of Shubenacadie, N. S., farmer, d May 1, 1857. Children:

1 Shelomeith, d unmarried in Australia.

2 Azael B.

3 William J.

Lavinia, m Ebenezer J. Pickings, Cal.

Kate H., unmarried, Cal.

4 Leander B.

5 Ethan Allen.

6 Richmond.

Lella W., m Forrest Foot, Cal.

3111132 AZAEL B., m Carrie Fisher, moved to California.

3111133 WILLIAM J., farmer, m Elizabeth Talbot, Shubenacadie, N. S.

3111134 LEANDER B., m in California.

3111135 ETHAN ALLEN, m Matilda Wright, Cal.

3111136 RICHMOND, unmarried.

31112 BENJAMIN, b probably about 17[illegible]2, in Nova Scotia; settled at Lebanon, Ct., where he d Aug., 1828.

[illegible]

Harvey (212247) say... that Benjamin and two brothers came from Wales.

3122 PELEG, b at Lebanon, Ct., 22, 1730, [illegible] m Mary Tyrrell, of Coventry, Ct., daughter of Col. Tyrell, who came from New Jersey, and who [illegible] Mass. PELEG was a soldier in the French War, [illegible] lived at Coventry, Ct., d [illegible].

Tryphena, b May 1, 25, 1751, m Abel Brown.
Ebenezer, b Sept. 12, [illegible], m [illegible], left a large family.
Anna, b Feb. 16, 1777, m A. Borriste[illegible].

1 Ezekiel, b Dec. 22, 1755.
2 Daniel.
3 Asa.
Sybil, m John White, moved to Ashtabula, O.
4 James, b July 8, 176[illegible].
5 Arad, b April 6, 176[illegible].
6 Charles.
7 Chester.

31221 EZEKIEL, b at Lebanon, Ct., Dec. 22, 1755, farmer, m [illegible] Lyon, settled in Harpersfield, O. Served as a private in the Revolution, d 1[illegible]. Had a large family of children, all of whom are dead.

31222 DANIEL, was a Revolutionary soldier, [illegible] was brutally murdered after the surrender of the fort near New London.

31223 ASA, [illegible] Revolutionary [illegible] W[illegible]

31224 JAMES, b [illegible], Ct., July 8, 1[illegible] [illegible] Harvey [illegible] He

[illegible]
b [illegible] Children—
1 Rowland.
2 James.
3 Justus.
4 [illegible] N., b [illegible]
5 Lysander C.
6 Luther P.
7 Harvey.
Sarah, m A[illegible], farmer, Shelburne, Mass.
Asenath, m Elijah Smith, farmer, Wayne Co., N. Y.
Lucretia, m Sylvester Smith, farmer, Wayne, Iowa.
Emily, m Carl Bishop, merchant, Shelburne Falls, Mass.
Dorcas, m Marcus Miller, farmer, Ma[illegible], O.
Tirzah, m Harry Wood, saddler.

312241 ROWLAND, mason, Berlin, Green Lake Co., Wis., m Ruth Moore.

312242 JAMES, farmer, Wayne, O., m Thankful Ellis. Children—
1 Ellis.
2 Baxter.
3 Omri.
4 James.

312243 JUSTUS, Methodist minister at Monmouth, Ill., in 1875, m Annie Breakman. Children—
1 Philander.
2 Scott.
3 Rowland.
4 John B.

312244 PARMENAS NEWTON, b June 30, 18[illegible], carpenter, Stony Point, Sonoma Co., Cal., m Martha McDonald. Children—
1 Lysander Catlin.
2 Darius.
Martha, m Isaac Fuller, Stony Point, Cal.
Mary, m Amasa Morse.
3 Abijah S.
Sarah, m George Hamilton, farmer, Stony Point, Cal.
Eliza, m Renshaw Wilson, bookkeeper, Petaluma, Cal.
Emily, m Madison B[illegible], San Francisco, Cal.
4 Charles W.
5 Samuel, b 1842.

312441 LYSANDER CATLIN, San Francisco, Cal., m Cynthia [illegible]

[illegible] DANIEL [illegible] Wor[illegible]
[illegible]
Anne M[illegible]
C[illegible]
1 [illegible]

312243 ARTEMAS [illegible] Chelsea.
1 Frederick.
2 Ralph.

312244 CHARLES W., S[illegible], Cal.

312245 SAMUEL, b 1852, [illegible] farmer, T[illegible], Cal.

312245 LYSANDER C., farmer, m 1st, S[illegible] Austin; 2d, Polly Cumming; lives at North Madison, Lake Co., O.

312246 LUTHER PORTER, farmer, Warren, Jo Daviess Co., Ill., m M. Babb.

312247 HARVEY, b at Bolton, Warren Co., N. Y., 1804, mason and farmer; m Sarah Kelsey, resided in 1876 at Painesville, O.; a most genial and hospitable old gentleman.
Emma, m S. C. Carter, Keokuk, Iowa.
Jennie S., m Lyman Beach, Mercer, Mercer Co. Pa.
Lucretia, unmarried.
1 Ralph D., unmarried, Painesville, O.
Harvey writes, "The Woodworth family will compare favorably with the rest of mankind," and then, as if in proof of the statement he adds, "I am an old line Whig, but voted for Horace Greeley in 18[illegible]."

31225 ARAD, b at Coventry, Ct., April 6, 17[illegible]8, settled in Warren, Mass., in 17[illegible]9, carpenter and builder; m Deborah Stanley, Hanover, Mass., d July, 1875, at Worcester, Mass. Children—
Arad, b 1791, d 1804.
1 Harvey, b 1795.
Laura, b 17[illegible] m Sewell Sargent, Leicester, Mass.
[illegible], m Abner L. Blair, moved to Rome, N. Y., d 18[illegible], left six children.
2 George C., b 1[illegible], d 1[illegible]8.
3 Ja[illegible] [illegible] Oct. [illegible]
4 A[illegible], b Dec. [illegible]
Mary, b Aug. 1[illegible], 1[illegible] m H[illegible] A[illegible], d 1836.
Harriet, b Nov. [illegible] m [illegible]
5 Peregrine Stanley, b Feb. 22, 1[illegible]
6 [illegible], b 1[illegible], d 1[illegible]2.

3 Lewis M.
4 Charles S.
5 Harvey.
6 Benjamin S.
Caroline.
7 Marcus M., d.
8 James S.

312511 ABEL, carpenter, Boston, Mass., m. Caroline Burd[illegible]. Children— Ida.

312512 DANIEL, carpenter, Warren, Mass., m. Ann Wh[illegible]. Children—
1 Samuel.
Fanny.
2 William.

312513 LEWIS M., carpenter, Olean, N. Y., m. [illegible] Mone. Children—
1 Frank.
One daughter.

312514 CHARLES S., carpenter, Boston, Mass., m. Mary Hodgers.

312515 HARVEY, tailor, Madison, O.

312516 BENJAMIN S., Warren, Mass.

312517 MARCUS, died in the army at Louisville, Ky.

312518 JAMES S., carpenter, Madison, O., m. Sevilla Miller. Children—
1 Charles S., Springfield, O.
2 Sewell S., Madison, O.
3 George W., Cleveland, O.

31225[illegible] JAMES S., b. at Warren, Mass., Oct. 10, 18[illegible]5, architect and builder, [illegible] Street, Worcester, Mass. He settled in Worcester in 18[illegible] and has ever since been identified with its growth and prosperity. He has been honored by various offices of the city government [illegible] and the State Legislature, and for many years [illegible] tor of the Worcester Mutual [illegible] He married [illegible] Stowell, who died in 18[illegible]; and [illegible] his second wife [illegible] Brigham, of Marlborough, Mass. Children—
1 George C., b. Aug. 18[illegible]1, d. 1878.

[illegible]

2 [illegible]

[illegible] dren [illegible]

[illegible] Wayne, [illegible]

312[illegible] JAMES [illegible] He was [illegible] the [illegible] Wayne, Ind., and [illegible] married Martha Mo[illegible], daughter of Judge John M[illegible], of Fort Wayne. Children—

Alice, b 1868.

1 Edward James.

2 Charles Stowell.

Theresa.

312254 ABAD, b at Warren, Mass. Dec. 1[illegible], 18[illegible]7, carpenter, Madison, O., m Sarah [illegible] Burgess. Children

1 John.

2 Norval.

Emma.

3 George Clinton.

Miriam.

3122541 JOHN, b at Leicester, Mass., m Adelaide Shaw, lives in Madison, O. Children—

1 Alfred E.

Lena.

Sarah.

2 Frank.

3 Henry.

Grace.

Nerval.

3122542 NORVAL, b at Leicester, Mass., m Mattie Allen, lives at Woonsocket, R. I. Children—

1 Burchard Allen.

3122543 GEORGE C., b at Leicester, Mass., m C. McGlynn. Children—

Nellie E.

Alice Winnifred.

Mamie Edith.

312255 BENJAMIN [illegible], b at Leicester, Mass., Feb. 1[illegible], 18[illegible], [illegible] at [illegible] Mass. [illegible] 18[illegible]

[illegible]

[illegible]

[illegible] A. W[illegible] who [illegible] Dr. [illegible] Woodworth [illegible] to be descended from [illegible] W[illegible] [illegible] brother [illegible] in New York. [illegible] It is [illegible] given it.

William

1

S[illegible]h.

1

Amos.

1

William, Luke, [illegible], Solomon.

1

Gersh[illegible], b 174[illegible], Montgomery Co., N. Y., Capt. in French and Indian Wars.

1

Ge[illegible] Evarts, b 175[illegible], Montgomery Co., N. Y., [illegible] Revolutionary war. [illegible]

1

[illegible], farmer and clergyman [illegible] M. E. [illegible], d [illegible] Middlebury, Vt., April, [illegible], his children were—

[illegible]

[illegible] Cal.

[illegible]

[illegible] G. H. [illegible]

[illegible] Children—

[illegible]

[illegible]

[illegible]

[illegible]

[illegible]

[illegible] by Mr. D. A. [illegible] W[illegible].

C[illegible] Co., [illegible]

[illegible] W. [illegible]

My [illegible]

[illegible]

D. A. Woodworth's [illegible] grandfather and my own grand-father was the same person "Gershom Woodworth." His eldest son was [illegible] Woodworth. He [illegible] son Ira whose son was [illegible] Ira [illegible]; his son was named Dorus Augustus. Gershom Woodworth, D. A. W.'s great great grand-father had [illegible] brothers [illegible] sisters. I speak of [illegible] I have [illegible]—William, [illegible], Benjamin, Abraham, Selah, [illegible] in Connecticut and Solomon, who was a captain and killed in the Indian war of "55." I never saw [illegible]. "Gershom", also had three sisters—[illegible] married a [illegible]-field, the other two I never saw, and have forgotten who they married. My name is William G., the son of William G., who was the second son of Gershom. My information as [illegible] down to me may differ from yours. It is this: Some time after the first landing of the Mayflower at Plymouth Rock, two Woodworths came from England and landed and settled at or near the same place with their families; about ten years after their younger brother and wife came over and settled near them; his name was Walter—afterwards he moved to the Province of Connecticut, and built the first [illegible] in the province. D. A. W.'s direct line is not from Walter but from [illegible], his elder brother.

Very respectfully, your friend,

W. G. WOODWORTH.

Solomon Woodworth, the son of [illegible] Woodworth, is described in [illegible] of [illegible], pages [illegible].

[illegible] party [illegible]

[illegible]

[illegible] Woolworth's own [illegible] of the savages [illegible] upon whom he fired [illegible] one of them [illegible] subsequently appeared [illegible] wounded. This [illegible] the Indians to retire. But Woolworth was not satisfied. Collecting half a dozen [illegible] he [illegible] close to the intruders and after [illegible] three days [illegible] overtook them—they having halted to dress the wound of their companion. The pursuit came so suddenly upon them, as to succeed in dispatching the whole number without allowing them time to offer resistance. The little band returned to Johnstown in triumph; and their leader was immediately commissioned a Lieutenant in a regiment of nine-months men, in which service he had again an opportunity of showing his prowess, as will be seen hereafter."

(Pages 163 and 164 same book). "The name Solomon Woolworth has twice or thrice occurred in the preceding pages; once as having been taken a prisoner and making his escape, and again as alone defending a block house north of Johnstown and repulsing the enemy from his fortress. In the year, 1781, he was commissioned a captain, for the purpose of raising a company of rangers to traverse the wooded country north of Fort Dayton and the German Flats. He succeeded in enlisting a company of forty brave and kindred spirits; at the head of whom, well armed and provided he marched from Fort Dayton, striking in the direction of the Royal Grant for purposes of observation. After a few hours march [illegible] of Woolworth's men, being a short distance in advance, discovered an Indian [illegible] whom he immediately fired. Instantly, the forest resounded with the war whoop, and Woolworth, with his little corps [illegible] surrounded by double his own number. [illegible]

[illegible]

31. 34 CHARLES [illegible] Wy[illegible]

[illegible]

21.26 [illegible] Jan. 11, 1798 [illegible] had nine children whose names are unknown.

32 JOHN, b. at Scituate Aug. 3, 17[illegible] Mary Rose Dec. [illegible] They had one child—

1 John, b. at Scituate Sept. 7, 17[illegible]

33 EBENEZER, b. at Scituate, Aug. 1[illegible], 1690, m. Mary Wade, Oct. 16, 1712. The following were born at Scituate:

Eleanor, b. Jan. 24, 1713.

Margaret, b. May 11, 1718, m. Thomas Webb, 1747.

Hannah, b. May 7, 1725.

ELEANOR, above named, m. Joseph Nottry Sept. 13, 17[illegible], and had 9 children, the oldest of whom Joseph, died soon after his [illegible] Betty, his widow, m. Benjamin Woodworth [illegible] of Samuel, the poet.

---

4 JOSEPH, son of Walter, Sr., b. at Scituate, m. [illegible] daughter of Charles Stockbridge, who kept the mill at Scituate [illegible] Children born at Scituate—

1 Joseph, b. March 2[illegible]

Margaret, [illegible] Stephen [illegible]

2 [illegible]

[illegible]

[illegible]

[illegible]

[illegible]

[illegible]

JOSEPH [illegible]

41 JOSEPH, b [illegible] M[illegible] 19, 167[illegible] m 16[illegible] [illegible] Little Compton, R. I., where his two children were born. He afterward moved to [illegible], Ct., where he owned [illegible], in 17[illegible], as appears from the [illegible] of a deed by him to his sons. Children—

1 Joseph, b March 17, 1[illegible]. Little Compton records.

2 Jedediah, b Dec. 1, 1[illegible]. Little Compton records.

411 JOSEPH, b at Little Compton, R. I., March 17, 1[illegible], m Ann Manchester Oct. 17, 172[illegible] moved to Lebanon, Ct., 17[illegible]. Children—

1 Abner, b Aug. 2, 1724.

Judith, b Feb. 4, 1726, m Adams Pierce May 13, 174[illegible].

Ruth, b Jan. 23, 1728, m Caleb Fitch April 4, 1747.

Sarah, b March 19, 1729, m Samuel Goodwin Oct. 24, 1745.

2 Walter, b 1731.

3 Zebedee, b 1733.

4 Lemuel, b June 25, 1735.

4111 ABNER, b at Little Compton, Aug. 2, 1724, m 1748, Hannah Dyer, of Norwich, Ct., and settled in Salisbury, Ct., where they had ten children. His wife died before 1790, and he then made his way alone on foot to Pompey, Yates Co., N. Y., carrying with him his kit of shoemaker's tools, and driving a cow. Two of his sons and two of his daughters soon joined him. He died in 1809, aged 84 years, at the home of his daughter, Molly. Children—

1 Elisha, b 1751.

2 Dyer, b Oct. 20, 1757.

3 Joseph, b Oct. 18, 1759, m Sarah Harding.

Sarah M., b Oct. 18, 1759, m Stephen Allen.

Eunice, b Nov. 22, 1762, m Timothy Sweet Sept. 14, 1780; lived at Pompey, N. Y.

Rebecca, m ——— Griswold.

4 Samuel, b Nov. 6, 1771.

Molly, b 1752, m Levi Benton, Sr., Pompey, N. Y.

Hannah, b June 18, 1754, m Gideon Woolcott, Sr., d April 16, 1842, at Coxsackie, N. Y.

Anna, b 1775, m 1st John Stevens; 2d, Nathaniel Keeler.

41111 ELISHA, b 1751 at Salisbury, Ct. He went in 1798 with his two sons, [illegible] and Elisha, to Pompey, Yates Co., N. Y., where he cleared eight acres on the farm now owned by John Merryfield, sowed it with wheat and returned to Salisbury. The next January he took with him to Pompey, his wife and children and settled there. Elisha m Ann [illegible], of [illegible] Co., N. Y., June 11, 1776. He died in 1805, his wife died in 18[illegible]. Children—

Polly, b Sept. 6, 1778, m Dr. Calvin Fargo in 1809, was living in

[illegible] Conn.
1 [illegible]
2 [illegible]
Sarah, [illegible] Penn Yan, [illegible]
2 [illegible]
[illegible] 182[illegible]
Amy, [illegible] 178[illegible] Washington [illegible]
Conn.
[illegible] Penn Yan.
Pamela, [illegible]

41111 ERASTUS B., b. at Salisbury, Ct., May 12, 17[illegible], [illegible] m. Olive, widow of Jonas Barden and sister of [illegible] and Dr. Walter Wolcott. He settled at [illegible], N. Y. Was surgeon of the [illegible] N. Y. Regiment, War of 1812. Was [illegible] and Justice of the Peace for several years. His children, [illegible], Hector and [illegible] all dead.

411112 ELISHA, b. at Salisbury, Ct., Aug. 16, 1781, school teacher. He went to Yates Co., with his father in 1799, m. Sarah K[illegible], settled at Benton, N. Y. Elisha's children were:
Harriet, m. Edward Perry.
1 Ariel.
Jane, m. Rowland Perry, Grand Blanc, Mich.
Catharine, m. ——— Bates, Grand Blanc, Mich.

4111121 ARIEL, b. about 1812 in Yates Co., N. Y., m. Miss Benton. [illegible] at Grand Blanc.

411113 ABNER, 2d, b. at Salisbury, Ct., May 13, 1785, m. in 1818, Isabella Place, of Seneca. Settled at Penn Yan, N. Y. Abner was a very [illegible] and popular man. Was Justice of the Peace, twenty-four years; Supervisor, two years; County Clerk, three years; candidate of the Whig party for Congress in 1842, was a captain in [illegible] N. Y. [illegible] in the War of 1812. He died in 18[illegible].

41112 [illegible], b. Oct. 26, 17[illegible], at Salisbury, Ct., was a [illegible] and [illegible] of [illegible]. In 179[illegible] he moved to Yates Co., N. Y., and in 1[illegible], [illegible] to the west [illegible] of the [illegible] River, Ind. Children —
[illegible], Benton, N. Y.
[illegible], [illegible].
[illegible].
[illegible].
1 Riley.
2 [illegible]

[illegible] LILY [illegible] of W[illegible] [illegible]

[illegible] ABRAHAM [illegible] Polly S[illegible] [illegible]

[illegible] SAMUEL, b. at [illegible], Nov. [illegible], 17[illegible] [illegible] daughter of Dr. [illegible] children.

Lucy, m. [illegible]

Eunice and [illegible]

Samuel.

Fanny.

SAMUEL m. a second time, Ann Sp[illegible] of Pompey, N. Y. By her he had three children:

Laura, b. at Pompey, Dec. 18, 18[illegible], m. Feb. 12, 1823, Hiram Sutherland, farmer, Pompey, N. Y.

Theodore, b. at Pompey, Mar. 1, 18[illegible], m. June 9, 1833, J[illegible] W[illegible], Battle Creek, Mich.

Helen Cola[illegible], b. Dec. 16, 1816, m. Dec. 10, 1835, Charles Campbell of Battle Creek, Mich.

SAMUEL m. the third time [illegible], sister of his second wife, Feb. 22, 18[illegible]. SAMUEL lived at Pompey 6 years; was a Member of Assembly in 1[illegible]2. He moved to Harmony, Ind., where he lived [illegible] years; afterwards lived at Princeton, Ind., and finally at S[illegible], N. Y., where he died Aug. 24, 1[illegible]57. His widow was living in 1[illegible] and is described as a remarkably handsome woman and one of the most active and delightful old ladies of 87 ever seen. They had four children:

1 A[illegible] Sprague, b. Mar. 12, 18[illegible].

F[illegible] Malvina, b. Feb. 2, 1[illegible], m. J. D. Wood, farmer.

2 William M[illegible], b. July 1[illegible], 18[illegible].

Sarah Augusta, b. July 19, 1[illegible], m. Feb. 7, 1[illegible]54, Lyman Dwight, Jr., Battle Creek, Mich.

[illegible] [illegible] SPRAGUE, b. at Pompey, [illegible] May 27, 1[illegible]. [illegible] of [illegible], Eng. Lived at [illegible] N. Y. [illegible] and S[illegible], N. Y. [illegible] Dec. [illegible] Sept. 2[illegible] [illegible] W. [illegible]

William [illegible], b. M[illegible] [illegible] June 22, 1[illegible]2

1 A[illegible], b. May 2[illegible]

[illegible], b. May 11, 1[illegible]57

[illegible]
3 [illegible]

[illegible] WILLIAM [illegible] [illegible] Feb. 12, 1853 [illegible] Williamsport, [illegible] N. Y. [illegible] WILLIAM M. [illegible] N. Y. Children—

Willie M., b [illegible], d July, 1856.
1 Charles S., b May 3, 1857.
2 Elmer S., b Feb. 28, 1861.
Jennie L., b Aug. 16, 186[illegible], teacher, Williamsport, Oswego Co., N. Y.
Claribel, b Aug. 10, 18[illegible], d Aug. 6, 1876.
After his wife's death WILLIAM M. [illegible] G. Rose, Mar. 2, 1878 and resides at Grayling, Crawford Co., Mich.

41111 CHARLES S., b May 3, 1857; telegraph operator, Detroit, Mich.

4111122 ELMER S., b Feb. 2[illegible], 1861, m Jennie E. [illegible] at Benton, Butler Co., Kansas; R. R. station agent and telegraph operator. Children—
1 Charles William, b [illegible] 1886.

4112 WALTER, b at Little Compton, R. I., 1736, moved to Lebanon, Ct., in 1754; m 1755, Rachel French, of Lebanon; he d Sept. 15, 1805. Rachel d Jan. 25, 1797. Children—
1 Jeduthon, baptized 1762.
Henan, b 1761, d 1784 at Port au Prince, unmarried.
2 Asahel, b 1759.
Lucy, b 1774, d Aug. 20, 1826.
Olive, b 1770, d Mar. 21, 1789, m Mr. Dimbleby.
Rachel, b———, d Nov. 25, 1790.

41121 JEDUTHON, b about 1761, m Feb. 20, 1798, Elizabeth Strong, d of Jedediah Strong, b Mar 25, 1769. Children—
Olive, b Jan. 15, 1801, m David C. Wolcott.
1 John M., b June 29, 1799.
2 H[illegible], b June 7, 1803.
3 David S., b Sept. 12, 1807.

41211 JOHN M., b June 29, 1799, m Mary W. A[illegible] Jan. 1, 18[illegible]. Blacksmith and farmer. He [illegible] a year. [illegible] Capt. [illegible] Woolworth, [illegible] Co. Children—
[illegible], b [illegible] 23, 18[illegible]

1 Mary [illegible]
[illegible]
b. [illegible], d. Jan. [illegible]
2 John, b. [illegible]
[illegible]
[illegible]
[illegible]
[illegible]
[illegible]
from the church [illegible]
for much of this history.

4112111 HENRY DWIGHT, b. at [illegible] Feb. 18, 1826, A. B. [illegible] Col. [illegible] 26, 1855, m. Apr. 17, [illegible] 55, Sarah E. [illegible]. He was a Congregational minister at Rehoboth. Children:
1 Horace Singleton, b. May 4, 1856, b. [illegible]
2 Henry [illegible], b. July 1, 1861.
3 James Armstrong, b. Sept. 28, 18[illegible].

411212 HEMAN, b. June 17, 1803, m. Mary Wyles. Children:
Caroline L., b. [illegible] 29, joined Franklin Church, May 7, 1843, m. Nov. 12, 1854 George W. Loomis, Norwich, d. Jan. 23, 18[illegible]7. Child—
1 George H.

4112121 GEORGE H., b. at Franklin, Ct., joined Franklin Church, May 7, 1843. Carriage maker, lives at Norwich, Ct.

411213 DAVID S., b. Sept. 12, 1807, at Lebanon, m. Sophia H. Bailey, Sept. 2[illegible], 1831. In [illegible] he was still living at Lebanon, a genial and very much respected old gentleman. He had no children.

41122 ASAHEL, b. at Lebanon 1753, m. Faith or Phebe Strong, Jan. [illegible] 1786. Children—
Asahel, d. unmarried.
Robert, d.
Walter, d. without children.
[illegible], m. Fred Ham, No. 21 E. 32 st., N. Y., [illegible] 1876.
Lucy.
Esther.

4112 [illegible], b. at Little Compton 17[illegible].

4111 [illegible], b. at [illegible], Ct., [illegible]
[illegible]. Children—
1 J[illegible]
2 [illegible] 1760.

[illegible]

[illegible]

[illegible]

[illegible]

3 [illegible]

4 [illegible]

[illegible]

[illegible] JOSEPH, [illegible] May [illegible] [illegible] Revolutionary War and [illegible] farmer [illegible] N. Y. [illegible] Napoli, Cattaraugus Co., N. Y. [illegible] Sally [illegible]

1 Luther.

2 Erastus.

3 Anson.

4 Abel.

5 [illegible]

His wife Sally [illegible] married Mary Parks and had [illegible] children.

6 William.

7 Hiles.

8 Jefferson.

9 Madison.

10 Joseph.

Sarah, m. —— —— Van Dusen, Painesville, O.

Polly.

Emmeline, m. Perry Barnum, Napoli, N. Y.

Caroline, m. Chauncey Bushnell.

Diana.

[illegible] LUTHER, [illegible] N. Y., farmer, m. Nancy Coase, had one son and [illegible] other children.

1 Harvey, [illegible] Apr. 26, 1811.

[illegible] HARVEY, b. at [illegible], N. Y., April [illegible], m. Emily [illegible] [illegible] Wis. [illegible] Fond du Lac [illegible] at [illegible], N. Y. Children.

[illegible] Sept. 28, [illegible], m. Thomas C. Maxwell, [illegible]

1 Willard [illegible] 15 [illegible]

May [illegible] Oct. [illegible] Dec. 17, 1874 [illegible] Unity, Wis.

[illegible] Fond du Lac [illegible] 1867.

2 John [illegible] Sept. [illegible] 3.

[illegible]

41312 [illegible]

1 [illegible]
  [illegible]
  [illegible]
2 [illegible]
3 [illegible]
4 [illegible]
  Harriet.
  Mary.
5 Charle[illegible]y.

41341[illegible] ALANSON, b. [illegible] Co., N. Y., farmer, was [illegible] member of Assembly in [illegible], and held other civil and military offices. His first wife was Mary Dickinson; his second was Nancy Dickinson. Children:
1 Anson, killed in the Battle of the Wilderness in 186[illegible], aged 24. He left a widow and one child living in Seneca Co., N. Y.
  Sarah, m. Leroy [illegible], Clinton, Iowa.
  [illegible], m. John [illegible], farmer, Wayne Co., N. Y.
  [illegible], m. Dr. John [illegible], [illegible], N. Y.
  [illegible], m. C. L. [illegible], [illegible], Mich.
  Mary A., m. H. S. [illegible], editor, St. Louis, Mo.
2 [illegible], unmarried, St. Louis.
3 [illegible] H.

4134[illegible] [illegible], b. in Seneca Co., N. Y., President and [illegible] of [illegible] [illegible] Company, St. Louis, Mo., m. Mary [illegible] of Seneca Co., N. Y. Children:
  Maud M.
  Grace [illegible]
  [illegible] [illegible]s.

4135[illegible] AUGUSTUS, b. in Seneca Co., N. Y., was [illegible] Loo[illegible].

41[illegible] A[illegible]N, [illegible] 18[illegible].

[illegible] N. Y.

[illegible]

[illegible] LUCAS [illegible] Co., N. Y. [illegible]

[illegible]

[illegible] N. Y.

2 [illegible] J.

3 [illegible]

[illegible] N. Y.

[illegible] N. Y.

[illegible] [illegible] J. [illegible] N. Y., m Francis J. [illegible] Children—

[illegible] F.

Sadie.

[illegible] ALBERT M., b at [illegible] N. Y. Congregational [illegible] Cumberland St., Brooklyn, L. I., m Sarah A. Temple. Child—

Clifford [illegible] deceased.

[illegible] LEMUEL, b at [illegible] N. Y.

[illegible] WILLIAM, b at [illegible] N. Y. m [illegible] Lucena [illegible], farmer, Ellsworth, Wis. Children—

1 Milton Case.

2 Francis D.

Alvira, m Richard McElwen, druggist, Ellsworth, Wis.

3 William Dempster.

Ella W., m Selah Strickland, Ellsworth.

Flora E., d at Windham, O., Oct. [illegible]

[illegible] MILTON CASE, physician, m Lizzie Bradley, had one son, d in 1861.

[illegible] [illegible] D., lawyer, Youngstown, O., was a member of Congress in 18[illegible]; m Celia A. Clark. Children—

[illegible]

[illegible]

[illegible] L.

[illegible] L.

[illegible] WILLIAM DEMPSTER, m Mary [illegible]

[illegible]

[illegible] HILON, went to [illegible]; is dead.

[illegible]

[illegible]

41142 BENJAMIN, b. [illegible] Zebedee [illegible] N. Y. [illegible] Children —

1 Benjamin.
2 Zebedee.
3 Hiram.
4 George.
Melissa, single.
Clarissa, [illegible] d. [illegible] 79.
Betsy.
Asenath.
Sally.
Sophronia, single.

411421 BENJAMIN, m. Children —

1 Merrill, Meadville, Pa.
2 Jerome.
Clarissa, m. Chas. Hutchinson, d. at Clarksville, N. Y., 1878.
A daughter m. --- Larkin, Jamestown, N. Y.

411422 ZEBEDEE, m. Children —

1 George, West Randolph, N. Y.
2 Charles, West Randolph, N. Y.
3 Spencer, Fort Dodge, Iowa.
Sophia, widow, West Randolph.
Susan, widow, Va.

411423 HIRAM, m., deceased. His widow lives at Wayland, O. Children —

1 Warren, [illegible], Iowa.
A daughter, m. Mr. Wadsworth, Wayland, O.
A daughter, m. Frederick Seldon, Russellsville, N. Y.
Helen.

[illegible] [illegible], N. Y. [illegible]
[illegible] Children —

1 [illegible], [illegible], N. Y.
2 [illegible].
3 [illegible], [illegible], N. Y.
4 [illegible], [illegible], N. Y.
5 George, [illegible], N. Y.
[illegible]

[illegible]

[illegible]

[illegible] N. Y. [illegible]

[illegible]

A. M., 18[illegible] [illegible] N. Y.

41143 LEMUEL, b. at Lebanon, Ct., July 15, 17[illegible], [illegible] N. Y., [illegible] to New York City. [illegible]
1 Lemuel.

4114[illegible] JOHN, b. at Lebanon, Ct., Feb. [illegible], 177[illegible]. Children—
1 Daniel, b. [illegible], Auburn, N. Y.
2 Alva, Manlius, Onondaga Co., N. Y.
Mary, m. ——, merchant.
Polly, m. ——, barber.

---

412 JEDEDIAH, b. at Little Compton, R. I., Dec. 1, [illegible] m. [illegible], moved to Lebanon. They were members of the First Church of Lebanon and are buried in its churchyard. From their gravestone we learn that "he finished a most exemplary life Nov. 11, 1777 aged 78." Children—
Amy, b. at Little Compton, April 20, 17[illegible].
Constant, m. 1750, —— —— Atchison.
1 Benjamin.
The children of Constant were b. [illegible]—
Eleazer, b. Nov. 6, 1752.
Abigail, b. July 25, 17[illegible].
Samuel, b. May 20, 1756.
Benjamin, b. April 2, 17[illegible].
Mary, b. Nov. 15, 1762.
[illegible], b. May 23, 176[illegible].

4121 [illegible]

5 ISAAC [illegible]

[illegible] Norwich [illegible] History of Norwich [illegible] the Norwich records [illegible] to his descendants [illegible] He died April [illegible] children [illegible] 1727. [illegible]

1 Moses, b. about 1687.

2 Isaac, b. about 16[illegible].

3 Daniel.

4 David.

5 Joshua.

6 Stephen.

51 MOSES, b. about 1687 at Norwich, Ct. [illegible] estate in 17[illegible]; was admitted as a freeman [illegible] the region around Waterways Hill [illegible] with rattlesnakes and a bounty of 4d per [illegible] capture. In 1729 Moses killed 27 and in 1731 [illegible] the rewards of 25. The other brothers were [illegible] Moses m. Mehitable Gay, May 21, 1720. In the [illegible] a deed from Moses of Norwich dated Nov. [illegible] 171[illegible] [illegible] [illegible] part of a lot [illegible] Walter Woodworth [illegible] his property [illegible]

[illegible] June 3, 17[illegible].

[illegible] April 16, 17[illegible].

[illegible] Aug. [illegible]

[illegible] 17[illegible]

[illegible] 1727 [illegible]

[illegible]

[illegible]

1757 [illegible]

[illegible]

[illegible]

1 [illegible]

2 [illegible]

[illegible]

3 [illegible]

4 [illegible]

Zeruah, b Sept. 23, 17[illegible].

5 Nathan, b Sept. 16, 17[illegible].

Grace, bap [illegible] March [illegible]

Isaac left a will dated Dec. 7, 17[illegible], in which he mentions the four younger children by name and his wife, Mercy[illegible].

[illegible]21 ISAAC, b at Norwich, Ct., Oct. 30, 171[illegible], m Elizabeth Fox, Aug. 2[illegible], 17[illegible]. Children—

Lucy, b June 4, 1739.

1 Jabez, b May 4, 1741.

2 Douglas, b June 29, 174[illegible].

5211 JABEZ, b at Norwich, Ct., 17[illegible], m Mrs. Martha Fox, of New London, Nov. [illegible], 1762. Children—

Elizabeth, b Jan. 31, 176[illegible].

1 Douglas, b Dec. 6, 1765.

2 Isaac, b Feb. 15, 1768.

3 Jabez.

52111 DOUGLAS, b at Norwich, Ct., 1765, m Oct. 24, 1791, Charlotte, daughter of [illegible]. [illegible] is said to have removed to New York.

52112 ISAAC, b at Norwich, Ct., 1768, moved to Vermont, and died at Chelsea, Vt., 1847. He was a farmer, m. for his first wife Rebecca [illegible]; for his second Martha [illegible]. Children—

Betsey.

1 [illegible], b 1793.

[illegible]

Lucy.

2 [illegible], b at Chelsea, Vt.

3 John [illegible], at Chelsea, Vt.

[illegible]

5.1121 [illegible], b at Chelsea, Vt., 179[illegible] [illegible] removed to [illegible]. Children—

[illegible]

[illegible]

[illegible]

1 [illegible]

5.11.11 [illegible]

[illegible]

[illegible]

[illegible]

5.12 [illegible] Martha, and to Patty, Abigail, W[illegible], and L[illegible] Woodworth.

522 ASA, b at Norwich, Ct., 1716, m. Sarah ———, d at [illegible], Ct., April 2, 18[illegible]. Children—

1 Simeon, bap. Norwich, Sept. 9, 1765.

2 Amos, bap. Norwich, Sept., 17[illegible].

Sarah.

5221 SIMEON, bap. in Norwich Church Sept. 9, 1765; admitted to the church in 1787, m Mary H. Lord, July 7, 1789, joined Franklin Church by letter Sept. 12, 1792; his wife joined by profession Dec. 21, 1791. Children—

1 Simeon, bap. April 3, 1791.

Horatio, b June 22, 1795, d June 26.

Mary Lord, b May 30, 1797, bap. June 30.

Laura, b Dec. 7, 1799.

52211 SIMEON, bap. April 3, 1791, at Norwich Church, m Phebe ———, who was admitted to Norwich Church in 18[illegible].

I find in the records of South Coventry, Conn., records of the births of three children of Simeon and [illegible] Woodworth. The name of Simeon's wife in the Norwich records is [illegible] [illegible] the name "Lord" which was the name of Simeon's [illegible] mother, [illegible] that Simeon of Norwich [illegible] to Coventry [illegible] the father of the following children:

Mary Lord, b [illegible]

Sarah [illegible]

1 [illegible]

5222 AMOS, bap. in Norwich [illegible], Sept. 17[illegible], d March [illegible]

[illegible] Nova [illegible]

523 JOHN, b [illegible] May [illegible] 1778 [illegible]

[illegible]

524 THOMAS, b [illegible] 17, [illegible] 2, [illegible] Nova Scotia [illegible] 1760, where [illegible] N. S. [illegible] Mary [illegible] at [illegible] N. S. She d April [illegible], 18[illegible]. Children—

Elizabeth, b at Norwich June 2, 175[illegible], m Stephen Eaton of [illegible] Nov. [illegible] 1775. [illegible] d March 2[illegible], 18[illegible]

1 Oliver, b Jan. 19, 1756.

Huldah, b Oct. 11, 175[illegible], at Norwich, m Timothy Eaton, brother of Stephen Oct. 25, 1781; had seven children, d July 14, 18[illegible]7.

2 Nathan, b June 16, 1[illegible], d Feb. 8, 1781.

3 Levi, b Feb. 11, 176[illegible].

5241 OLIVER, b at Norwich Jan. 19, 1756, went to Nova Scotia with his father in 1760, m Ruth [illegible] April 25, 1782; she d and for his second wife m [illegible] Sept. 7, 1819; had one son—

1 Nathan, b about 1785.

52411 NATHAN, b in N. S. about 1785, m Sarah Baxter, daughter of Dr. Wm. Baxter, Feb. 24, 1805; she d April 6, 18[illegible], aged 4[illegible]. NATHAN m again Julia Baxter, sister of his first wife. He d July 22, 18[illegible]. Children—

1 Wm. Oliver, b July 18, 1808, single; was drowned.

Prudence Ruth, b June 8, 1810, d Aug. 31, 1812.

2 Benjamin Baxter, b May 15, 1812.

Ruth, b May 15, 1814, m John Cox.

Douglas, b Aug. 15, 1817, d Jan. 6, 1818.

Ruby, b June 1, 1819, m Newton Cox.

Sarah Eliza, m Levi W. Eaton, July 28, 1851.

3 Douglas S., b Feb. 19, 1821.

524112 BENJAMIN BAXTER, b May 15, 1812, in N. S., m March [illegible], 18[illegible] Emmeline [illegible]; she d Ap[illegible], aged [illegible]. Children—

Maria, b [illegible] 19, 18[illegible] [illegible] Oct. 27, 1862.

1 [illegible], b Ap[illegible] 25, 18[illegible]7.

[illegible], b Feb. 2[illegible], 18[illegible] [illegible] Oct. 2[illegible], 18[illegible].

2 Douglas Benjamin, b [illegible]

BENJAMIN m again April 24, 1845, Prudence [illegible], sister of his first wife. Children—

[illegible]

5 Benjamin Baxter, b. Apr. 15, 1875.

5[illegible]1 JOSEPH EDWARD, b. April 26, 1857, m. Nancy Cox, Mar. 7, 1883. Children —

1 John Frederick.

2 Benjamin Franklin.

62411[illegible] DOUGLAS BENJAMIN, b. June 2, 1840, m. Feb. 28, 1864, Elizabeth Churchill, of Hantsport, N. S. He was elected to the Local House from Kings Co. in 187[illegible], and continued to be a member until 1878. In June, 1882, he was elected to the Dominion Parliament of which he was a member until the general election in 1887. He has been a barrister since 186[illegible] and Queen's counsel since 18[illegible]. His place is in Halifax. Children —

1 Perry Churchill, studying medicine at Halifax.

2 Joseph Edward Todd.

62411[illegible]3 GEORGE WHITFIELD, b. Feb. 11, 1846; m. Minnie Churchill July 1, 1871. She d. leaving no issue. He then m. Sarah A. [illegible], of Long Island, N. S., May 3, 1875. Children —

1 Nathan Allen, b. March 21, 1877, at Canning, N. S.

2 Stafford Douglass, b. Dec. 10, 1878, at Kentville.

Prudence Rusby, b. Sept. 28, 1880.

Sarah Glee, b. Sept. 4, 1888.

[illegible] LEVI, b. Feb. 21, 1767, in N. S., m. Lydia Clark, Feb. 27, 1794. Children —

1 Thomas Douglas, b. April 28, 1[illegible], d. Feb. 17, 1827.

2 George, b. A[illegible] 2, 1796.

Lydia Matilda, b. Dec. 19, 1799.

Jo[illegible], b. Sept. 14, 18[illegible].

3 Levi Charles, b. June 26, 1808.

5[illegible] LEVI CHARLES, b. June 26, 1808, m. widow of John [illegible], Jan. 4, 1862. She d. June 28, 18[illegible], leaving one son —

1 Charles Levi.

525 NATHAN, b. at N[illegible], Ct., Sept. [illegible] 173[illegible], bap. Jan. 21, 1733; settled in Lyme, Ct., m. [illegible] Longbottom. Children —

1 Rial.

Holdah.

2 Nathan.

Ascathy.

Wealthy, named in will of Douglas (5212).

3 Isaac.

53 DANIEL, b. [illegible] m. Mehitable Brown, Norwich, Ct., Dec. 15, 1720. He owned large tracts of land in Connecticut Plains. Children —

1 Daniel, b. Aug. 20, 1721.

Mehitable, b. March 13, 1723.

2 Benjamin, b. Dec. 9, 1724.

Mary, b. May 10, 1726.

Anne, b. Dec. 28, 1727.

Joseph, b. Nov. 5, 1729, d. 1729.

Joseph, b. March 4, 1731, d. 1731.

3 William, b. Oct. 3, 1732.

4 Nathaniel, b. March 15, 1734.

Samuel, b. Aug. 8, 1739, d. 1739.

531 DANIEL, JR., b. at Norwich, Ct., Aug. 20, 1721, m. Sarah Collins 1740. Children —

1 Absalom, b. Aug. 13, 1741.

2 Robert, b. June 1[illegible], 1743.

3 Daniel, b. Jan. 13, 174[illegible].

5311 ABSALOM, b. at Norwich, Aug. 13, 1741; [illegible] in New York [illegible] merchant; d. [illegible], leaving no wife or children, Nov. [illegible], 17[illegible]. Letters of administration were granted by the Surrogate of New York to his brother Robert. I find in the records of the "[illegible] of Albany" mention of an Absalom [illegible] wife Catharine [illegible], who had one son Robert, b. at Albany, Nov. [illegible], 17[illegible].

5312 ROBERT, b. at Norwich, Ct., June 1[illegible], 174[illegible]; "Yeoman;" settled [illegible] Rensselaer Manor [illegible], Albany Co., N. Y. His wife's name was Rachel [illegible] [illegible]

[illegible]

1 John, b. Nov. 1[illegible], 17[illegible]

[illegible] JOHN, [illegible]

[illegible] New York [illegible]

[illegible] Spencer [illegible] Good [illegible]

he was [illegible] when he [illegible]. He was a [illegible], poetry [illegible] and [illegible] with cheerfulness [illegible].

He was [illegible] of speech and [illegible] popular [illegible]. In his [illegible] Troy he engaged in [illegible] the General Term of the [illegible] at Albany [illegible] 1, 1858 [illegible]. He wrote a small book [illegible] "Reminiscences of Troy," from which the above information is gathered. [illegible] following [illegible] "First Settlers of Albany": "Catherine Westerlo, b. Aug. 26, 1778 [illegible] John Woodworth [illegible] d. Sept. 27, 1846."

5312 DANIEL, b. at Norwich, Ct., Jan. 13, 1775.

132 BENJAMIN, b. at Norwich, Dec. 9, 1724; [illegible] July 11, 17[illegible]. At a meeting of the Governor and Committee of Safety held [illegible] May [illegible] 1782, Benjamin presented a memorial, showing that two of his sons were wounded at Groton Heights [illegible] the fort, and that he had been at great expense in nursing them, whereupon Capt. Perkins was ordered to deliver to him [illegible] barrel of [illegible], a barrel of beef, a barrel of flour and two gallons of rum. Mrs. Arnold Perkins, of Plainfield, Madison Co., N. Y., a granddaughter of Benjamin, informs me that he had [illegible] children, but the following are all the children whose names I have been able to learn:—

2 [illegible]

[illegible] m. Mr. S[illegible]

Sarah, m. Mr. Hawkins.

2 Jo[illegible]

3 [illegible]

4 [illegible]

[illegible]

5 [illegible]

[illegible]

5321 [illegible]

[illegible] JOSEPH [illegible]

5323 ZEBA[illegible] b at Norwich [illegible] April [illegible] [illegible] at the Battle of [illegible] Heights Sept. 6, 17[illegible] [illegible] [illegible] that if [illegible] he would have [illegible] [illegible] pital, where he [illegible] really recovered but was always lame. He bought lands and settled in Montpelier, Vt., where he became a devoted minister of the gospel in the Methodist Church. He was engaged to a beautiful girl named [illegible] who died on the eve of his final departure for Vermont.

5324 AZEL, b at Norwich, Ct., Aug. 6, 17[illegible]. He, too, was a soldier in the Revolution and, with his brother, was severely wounded at the Battle of Groton Heights, so that he was for many years a cripple. He m and had two children:

Phebe.

1 Joseph Elley, b at Groton, Ct., 1[illegible], d April 1[illegible], 18[illegible], at New London.

5326 SAMUEL, b at Norwich, Ct., June 27, 1[illegible]71; m at Bozrah, Ct., Abigail Gardner, who was b April 12, 1767, and d July 5, 18[illegible]; date of marriage, June 12, 179[illegible]. Samuel moved to Bridgewater, Oneida Co., N. Y., about 1794; was member of Assembly in 182[illegible]; d Oct. 10, 18[illegible]. Children:

1 Isaac, b April 13, 1791.

Elizabeth, b June 15, 17[illegible].

2 Samuel, b Sept. 9, 17[illegible].

3 [illegible], b Oct. [illegible] 17[illegible].

Amand[illegible], b May 15, 180[illegible]; m — Perkins, Brookfield, Madison Co., N. Y.

53261 ISAAC, b April [illegible], 17[illegible], at Bozrah, Ct.; m May 24, 1812, Har[illegible] Mills, who was b July 16, 17[illegible]. Isaac was a [illegible] and lived at Bridgewater, N. Y.; d May 11, 18[illegible]. [illegible] b at [illegible], [illegible] Co., N. Y.:

1 Samuel, b Feb. [illegible], 1[illegible].

2 William Wallace, b Jan. 1, 1817.

[illegible]

[illegible]

[illegible]

[illegible]

[illegible]

[illegible] N. Y.

[illegible] N. Y.

Caroline, b. at P[illegible], O[illegible] Co., N. Y.

6 Charles, b. at P[illegible] Co., N. Y.

532611 SAMUEL, b. [illegible] N. Y. [illegible] d. May [illegible] 18[illegible]7. Had [illegible] children.

532612 WILLIAM WALLACE, b. [illegible] at Columbus, [illegible] Co., N. Y.; m. first, Lucy [illegible]; m. [illegible] Herkimer Co., N. Y. [illegible] moved to Dubuque, Iowa, and later to St. Paul, Minn. Children —

By first wife —

Elvira, m. L. L. Wetmore, Dubuque.

By second wife —

Augusta, m. Dr. Reed, Dubuque.

1 George B., 253 Seminary ave., Chicago, Ill.

2 Byron.

532613 EPHRAIM, b. Oct. 23, 1826 at Columbus, N. Y., lives at Dubuque, Iowa.

532614 CHAUNCEY, b. April 7, 1828, at Columbus, N. Y., lives at [illegible], Minn. Had two children.

532615 GRANVILLE, b. 18[illegible] at Bridgewater, Oneida Co., N. Y., lives at Rochester, N. Y. Had three children.

532616 CHARLES, b. 1835 at Bridgewater, N. Y., lives at Bridgewater, N. Y.

623 WILLIAM, b. at Norwich, Ct., Oct. 3, 1732; bap. Jan. 21, 1733; m. Sarah [illegible], b. 1736. William removed to Cornwallis, N. S. in 17[illegible], [illegible] wife d. in 1767. Children —

Betsy, b. Sept. 15, [illegible] at [illegible], Ct.; m. May 14, 1772, J. Smith, of Newport, R. I.

1 William, b. Aug. 3, 17[illegible].

2 Timothy, b. Nov. [illegible], 17[illegible], [illegible], Ct.

3 Alexander, b. July 19, 17[illegible], at Cornwallis, N. S.

4 [illegible], b. Feb. 4, 17[illegible], at Cornwallis, N. S.

[illegible], b. [illegible], at Cornwallis, N. S.

5 [illegible], b. [illegible] 2, 17[illegible], at Cornwallis, N. S.

53II PETER, b. Dec. 2[illegible] 17[illegible]; m. Mary Kers[illegible] Dec. [illegible]

53f NATHANIEL, b. [illegible]wich, Ct., March [illegible], 172[illegible]; [illegible]

54f DAVID, [illegible] Church [illegible] City [illegible] of [illegible] May 1[illegible] 1724; lived in [illegible] Lebanon. Children —

Lydia, b. March 6, 1725.
1 Elijah, b. Sept. 25, 17[illegible].
Hannah, b. Sept. 8, 1728.
2 Elisha, b. May 2, 1730.
Jerusha, b. Oct. 20, 1732.
3 Ralph, b. April 15, 17[illegible].
4 David, b. Jan. 2[illegible], 1737.
Obedience, b. April 6, 1740.
Prudence, b. May 2[illegible], 1742.
5 Moses, b. March 7, 17[illegible].

54I ELIJAH, b. at Nor[illegible] Ct., [illegible] 25, 17[illegible]; d. in New [illegible] Ct., soon after the [illegible] Children:
1 Nathan, b. Aug. 2[illegible], [illegible].
2 Zilla,
[illegible] N. Y. 1[illegible]3.
[illegible]

54II NAT[illegible] Ct. [illegible], [illegible] was b. at [illegible] March [illegible] lived in [illegible] Vt., [illegible] Children —
1 Wal[illegible]
2 [illegible]
3 Nat[illegible]

[illegible]

[illegible] 12, 182[illegible].

54111 WALTER [illegible] Moses [illegible] wood worker, and [illegible] cheint. He resided at Cromwell, Ct., and afterward at [illegible] ville, N. C., where he d. Sept. [illegible] He m. [illegible] Mary S[illegible], b. at Cromwell, Ct., Oct. [illegible] 17[illegible]. She was crippled by [illegible] and was always [illegible] She was [illegible] woman and possessed [illegible] She d. [illegible] Mass., Jan. 26, 18[illegible].

Frances M., b. D[illegible] 2[illegible]; d. at New Haven, Ct., May 8, 1[illegible]
Nathan S., b. 18[illegible]; d. 18[illegible]7.

1 William W., b. Oct. 16, 1[illegible].
Marcia [illegible], b. Dec. 26, 18[illegible]; m. 18[illegible] [illegible] Grace, d. at West Hartford, Ct., July 4, 187[illegible], leaving three children.

2 James W., b. Jan. 14, 1822.
Mary S[illegible], b. Aug. 4, 18[illegible], at Middletown, Ct.; m. Jan. 12, 184[illegible], at New Haven, Ct., Harrison G[illegible], of [illegible], Mass., who d. [illegible] 18[illegible]. Mary [illegible] m. Oct. 18[illegible] [illegible] G. Daniels, of Clinton, W. Va. Mr. Daniels d. at Pomeroy, Ohio, Nov. 20, 1853. She [illegible] Mass.

541111 WILLIAM WALTER, b. at Cromwell, Ct., Oct. 16, 181[illegible]; graduated from Yale College 18[illegible], and from Andover Theological Seminary; was settled as pastor of the Congregational Church [illegible] Ct., in 18[illegible]; of [illegible] Congregational Church, Waterbury, Ct., 18[illegible]; of Congregational Church, [illegible] 1[illegible]; of Congregational Church, [illegible] 1[illegible]; of Congregational Church, [illegible] Mass., 1[illegible]; of Congregational Church, [illegible] 1[illegible]7[illegible] [illegible] 1876 [illegible] [illegible] [illegible] [illegible] [illegible] [illegible] [illegible] of Dr. [illegible] [illegible] of W[illegible] [illegible] [illegible] [illegible] [illegible] [illegible] [illegible] [illegible] [illegible] [illegible]

[illegible] Walter [illegible] S[illegible] [illegible] Ap[illegible] A. S[illegible] [illegible] Female Seminary, Lakesville, [illegible] of [illegible] Iowa [illegible] [illegible] which he died two days later, June 13, 18[illegible]. Children—

By first wife—

1 William A., b July 5, 1841.

By second wife—

2 Charles Goodrich, b Oct. 22, 1845, d Aug. 2, 1864.
  Walter, b Feb. 21, 1848, d Feb. 24, 1848.
  Sarah Goodrich, b Aug. 21, 1850.
3 Frank Goodrich, b Dec. 23, 1853.
  Mary Montague, b Dec. 7, 1855.
  Samuel G., b June 23, 1863, d May 7, 1858.

By third wife—

  Harrison Garfield, b Jan. 22, 1868, d May 1, 1867.
4 Robert Sessions, b Oct. 17, 1869.
5 Arthur Vine, b Oct. 21, 1872.
6 James Walter, b Jan. 5, 1875.

Lucy Atwater, first wife of Rev. Wm. W. Woodworth, was a daughter of Dr. Wm. Atwater and Harriet Pomeroy, and was born Sept. 16, 1813.

Wm. Atwater was a graduate of Yale, 1807, and settled as a physician at Westfield, Mass.; he m Dec. 20, 1810, Harriet Pomeroy; he was a son of Rev. Noah Atwater, a graduate of Yale, 1774, who settled in the ministry at Westfield, Mass.; he m Rachel Lyman, of Northampton. He was a descendant of David Atwater, of New Haven, Ct. (See Atwater genealogy.)

Harriet Pomeroy, wife of Dr. Wm. Atwater, was a daughter of Lemuel Pomeroy and Eunice Lyman, and was b. at Northampton, Mass., May 23, 1787. Her father, Lemuel, was 4th son of Gen. Seth Pomeroy and Mary Hunt. Gen. Pomeroy was a distinguished soldier in the Colonial wars, and at the breaking out of the Revolution was commissioned as Brigadier General of the Continental Army. He fought at the battles of Bunker Hill and Ticonderoga and Crown Point. He died in 1776. He was a grandson of Deacon Medad Pomeroy and Experience Woodward, who were married at Northampton in 1661.

[illegible] Wal[illegible] W[illegible] [illegible]

[illegible]

[illegible] M[illegible] [illegible]

1618.

[illegible] Wheat Marsh [illegible]

David [illegible]

Rev. [illegible] Oct [illegible] Katharine [illegible]

1759.

Rev. [illegible] Children—

Rev. Chauncey A., b 1759, m [illegible] Webster, sister of Noah Webster, L. L. D.

Rev. Elnathan, b 1757.

Rev. Samuel b 1763, m Elizabeth Ely, of Saybrook, "the handsomest woman in Connecticut." 1784.

The children of Rev. Samuel were—

Sarah Worthington, b 1785, m Hon. F. Wolcott.

Elizabeth, b 1787, m Rev. Noah Coe.

Abigail, b 1788, m Rev. Samuel Whittlesey.

Catharine, b 1791, m Daniel Dunbar, Esq.

Rev. Charles Augustus, b 1790, m Sarah Upson.

Samuel Griswold, b 1793, m Mary Boot. His literary name was "Peter Parley."

Mary Ann, b 1799, m Col. Nathaniel B. Smith, of Woodbury, Ct.

Emily Chauncey, b 1807, m Rev. Darius Mead.

The children of Rev. Charles Augustus Goodrich were—

Sophia, m John Ashton.

Sarah Upson, m W. W. Woolworth.

Arabella, m Benjamin Callendar.

Charles m Mary Ashton.

Samuel G., m Emily Butler

Katherine Chauncey, m Thomas Dutton, d 1836.

Frederick, d at Cape Colony, unmarried.

521111 WILLIAM ATWATER, b July 7, 1844, at Berlin, Ct., author of this genealogy, graduated from Yale College 1865, and from Albany Law School 1866. Lawyer residing at White Plains, Westchester Co., N. Y., m Dec. 28, 1871, Elizabeth K. Wills, daughter of O. B. Wills, Ph. D., of White Plains; lived at New Rochelle, N. Y., until 1875, and since that time at White Plains, N. Y. Children—

Amy Atwater, b at New Rochelle, July 2, 1875.

SARAH G., daughter of WILLIAM WATER, b at Berlin, Ct., Aug. 21, 1[illegible] m Dec. 10, 2[illegible] [illegible] Hartford, Ct.

[illegible]

[illegible]

[illegible], 1872.

[illegible]

[illegible], 1876.

MARY [illegible] WILLIAM WALTER [illegible] Dec. 7, [illegible] A. M. [illegible] tect. They live at [illegible], Iowa. They have two children—

Boyd

Ruby.

5411113 FRANK GOODRICH, b at Waterbury, Ct., Dec. 23, 1853; graduated from Iowa College 1875, A. M. 1879; studied theology at Hartford Seminary; settled over the Congregational Church at Wolcott, Conn., in 1880; m June 1, 1881, Ellen Evaline, daughter of Samuel Upson, of Kensington, Ct. In 1892 he was elected President of the Tougaloo University, Miss., an institution for the education of the colored race in the South; was a delegate to the Congregational Council at London, England, 1891. Has one child—

Bessie, b July 7, 1887.

5411114 ROBERT SESSIONS, b at Grinnell, Iowa, Oct. 17, 1869; A. B. Amherst, 1890.

5411116 JAMES WALTER, b at Grinnell, Iowa, Jan. 5, 1875; A. B., Amherst, 1896; lives at Clinton, Conn.

5411115 ARTHUR VINE, b at Grinnell, Iowa, Aug. 21, 1872; A. B., Amherst, 1892.

541112 JAMES WALLACE, b Jan. 14, 1822; was a young man of considerable musical ability and is the composer of a number of hymn tunes. The tune "Woodworth," commonly sung to the hymn, "Just As I Am," etc., was composed by him and sold to Wm. B. Bradbury, to whom the composership is generally, but erroneously attributed.

54112 ELIJAH, farmer, resided at Schroon Lake, Essex Co., N. Y., d 1836.

54113 NATHAN, captured near Fort Erie in the War of 1812 and never heard from.

5411 PHILO, resided at Wells, Vt., with his stepfather, W. Fisk, till he was of age; was a Methodist preacher; m Lucy Gasten Hall, of Pelham, Niagara Co., N. Y.; d Aug. 1871. Children—

[illegible], resides at Pelham, N. Y.

[illegible]

1 [illegible] [illegible] Valley, [illegible]

5412 [illegible] [illegible] [illegible] [illegible]

542 [illegible] [illegible] Carter [illegible]

543 [illegible] [illegible] 17[illegible] [illegible] Connecticut [illegible]

544 DANIEL, [illegible] [illegible] 173[illegible].

545 MOS[illegible] [illegible] [illegible] 7, 1[illegible]48.

---

55 JOSEPH[illegible] [illegible] Norwich, Ct. 17[illegible] [illegible] Children—

Ruth, b April 17, [illegible]

Martha, b May 10, 17[illegible] m Jonathan Harris Nov. 13, 1751.

1 Joshua, b Feb. [illegible], 1737, d March 19, 17[illegible].

Zipporah, b July 19, 1741.

1 Joshua, b Oct. 1[illegible], 174[illegible]

551 JOSHUA, b at Norwich, Oct. 1[illegible], 174[illegible], m Lucy Williams March 2[illegible], 1771; lived at Montville, Ct. Children—

Jerusha R., b Sept. 8, 1771, m Christopher Leffingwell.

Lucy, b Feb. 25, 1773, m John Avery March 17, 179[illegible].

Sarah, b Oct. 13, 1774, m Benjamin Adams.

Phebe, b July 23, 1776.

Nancy, b Nov. 14, 1778.

1 Russell, b Oct. 2[illegible], 1780.

2 Joshua Elliot, b Jan. 30, 1783.

3 Charles, b May 2, 1785, d unmarried.

Castinciana, b Oct. 16, 1787, m Frances Minor.

5511 RUSSELL, b at Montville, Ct., Oct. 29, 1780, m Sarah Story. Children—

1 Russell Hubbard, b 1802, d in infancy.

Lois, b 1[illegible]0[illegible], m Charles [illegible], d Feb. 16, 1848, at Delhi, N. Y.

Lucy, b 1812.

2 Elias, b 181[illegible].

Maria, b 181[illegible], m Ephraim Clark, Chester, N. J.

3 George, b 1823

4 W[illegible]

55112 ELIAS, b at Montville, Ct., 181[illegible] farmer, lives at East Great Plain, Norwich, Ct.; m Harriet Swan, Oct. 13, 1841.

1 [illegible] b 1[illegible], d 187[illegible]

2 [illegible], b Dec. 18[illegible]

551122 FRANK H., b at Montville, Ct., Dec. 1848, m [illegible] McD[illegible] 18[illegible]; [illegible] [illegible] [illegible] of the [illegible] of Wood

[illegible]

[illegible]

M[illegible], Gar[illegible]

55113 GEORGE, [illegible] Mc[illegible] [illegible]. Children—

Sa[illegible], b 18[illegible].

Ma[illegible], b 1874.

551[illegible] WILLIAM [illegible], Ct., m Julia A[illegible] [illegible] Delhi, N. Y. Children—

Mary, m Mr. Davis [illegible] Delhi.

Ella, m Mr. Naugh[illegible].

5512 JOSHUA ELLIOT, b Jan. [illegible], 17[illegible], m Nancy Wheeler, at Norwich, Ct., d July, 1850. Children—

1 Thomas B.

2 Joshua E.

Annie.

3 Ebenezer.

4 Charles.

Lucy, m Jared Gr[illegible]man.

Fanny M., b 182[illegible], m Wm. Peckham [illegible] 3, 18[illegible].

Mary, m Joshua B. Leffingwell, of [illegible], Feb. 15, 18[illegible].

Abby S., m Wm. B. [illegible] April 4, 1825.

Lydia, m Jerome W. Williams, Dec. 16, 1[illegible].

Harriet.

55121 THOMAS B., m (first) Mary Dolbe[illegible], (second) Lucy Williams; farmer, 85 W. Thames street, Norwich, Ct. Children—

1 Chauncey B., b 18[illegible], m Sarah H[illegible], cashier Norwich Savings Society, Norwich, Ct. Children—

Abby J.

55122 JOSHUA, E., m Sally Fitch, at Mansville, Ct., Nov. 2[illegible], 1831; had one child—

[illegible], now dead.

55123 EBENEZER, [illegible] Peckham, [illegible] Norwich; had one child—

Harriet Peckham.

55124 Charles, m Mary A[illegible] Feb. 7, 1[illegible]; had two children, one boy, one girl, who m Mr. [illegible].

— —

56 STEPHEN, m [illegible] [illegible] will [illegible] his wife [illegible] [illegible] dated [illegible] 17[illegible] [illegible]

[illegible]

[illegible]

[illegible]

[illegible]

1 [illegible]

2 [illegible]

3 [illegible] 7

4 Stephen, b. N[illegible]

Jemima, b. [illegible]

Al[illegible], b. Ap. 15, 1752.

561 JONATHAN, b. [illegible], Ct., Oct. 2, 1738, m. Mercy [illegible] of Wellington, Ct., Oct. 29, 1767, and d. [illegible]. Children—

1 Nehemiah, b. June 14, 1768.

2 Charles, b. May 13, 1770.

5611 NEHEMIAH, b. June 14, 1768, may have moved to Stonington, Ct., and be the ancestor of the family mentioned on page [illegible].

5612 CHARLES, b. May 13, 1770, carpenter, lived in Stafford, Ct., m. Mel[illegible], his cousin, d. in 1840. Children—

1 Rudolphus.

2 Jedidiah.

3 Charles.

4 Gurdon.

Mary, m. Dea. Walker.

56121 RUDOLPHUS was a lawyer, lived at Stafford, Ct., where he died.

56122 JEDIDIAH, farmer, at Stafford, Ct.

56123 CHARLES, b. at Stafford, Ct., 17[illegible]7, was a school teacher, also Col. of militia, and farmer; m. Lily Avery, lived at Stafford. Children—

1 Charles Louis.

Caroline L., m. Wm. King, M[illegible]son, Mass.

2 Sherman.

Eleanor A., m. [illegible], of Lockport, N. Y.

3 Giles.

4 Dexter S.

Emily L., m. C. R. [illegible], M[illegible], Mass.

561231 CHARLES LOUIS, b. at Stafford, Ct., [illegible]

[illegible]

[illegible] Children—

[illegible]

1 [illegible]

[illegible]

56211 [illegible]

56[illegible] [illegible]

[illegible]

56123 [illegible]

56122 GURDON, [illegible] Polly [illegible] at Franklin, Ct., Jan. 21, 1820, [illegible] again June 11, 1837, A. L. Manning, lived at W[illegible], Ct.

562 JESSE, b at Norwich, Ct., Dec. 8, 1740. His name appears [illegible] the Norwich records as Joseph, although the will of his father, Stephen, dated April 10, 1771, contains no mention of a son, Joseph, but does mention Jesse as his second son. He m Mabel Otis of New London April 3, 1762. Children—

1 Amasa, b March 13, 1764.

2 Dudley, b Dec. 9, 1766.

3 Guy.

4 Jesse.

Eunice, b May 20, 1774, m Gibson. Her descendants live at Willimantic. Ct.; one is Mrs. Merrick Johnson.

Clarissa, m July 6, 1794, Adonijah Foote, Springfield, Mass.

5621 AMASA, b at Norwich, Ct., March 13, 1764, m. Abigail Winship April 15, 1787, d Nov. 18, 1833 at Franklin. Abigail joined the Franklin Church "by profession" June 4, 1795, and on the same day her children, then living, were baptized. Children—

1 Stedman, b Oct. 12, 1787.

Polly, b Oct. 14, 1790.

2 Jesse, b March 12, 1792.

Mabel.

3 Dudley.

Abigail, bap. Sept. 16, 1798.

Laura, b Dec. 7, 17[illegible] bap. April 20, 1800.

56211 STEDMAN, b at Franklin, Ct., Oct. 12, 1787, m. Nancy Cardwell, of [illegible] Dec. 30, 1810. They had one child—

1 [illegible]

2 George R., b July 29, 18[illegible].

3 Charles S., d 1881.

4 William L., d [illegible].

[illegible]

[illegible] [illegible]

[illegible] Mo. [illegible]

[illegible] [illegible] Apr. [illegible] 1882 [illegible]

Margaret [illegible] N. Y. [illegible]

5622 [illegible] Ct., Dec. [illegible] 1766 [illegible] Mass. [illegible] Mary [illegible] Ct. [illegible] learned the trade at Norwich. [illegible] the Housatonic River, south of Great Barrington [illegible], by the use of water power, he was able to [illegible]. He afterwards bought the old [illegible] the [illegible] Mills, and were used for [illegible] plaster, and at a later day for [illegible] machines. Children—

1 Edward Park [illegible]

Harriet, b. Jan. [illegible], 1797, [illegible] of Salisbury [illegible] only son, E. P. Hanmen, lives at Columbus, O.

56221 EDWARD PARK [illegible], b. at Great Barrington, Mass., April 13, [illegible] m. Harriet Hudson Oct. 15, 1827, and d. Dec. 24, 18[illegible]. [illegible] Nov. [illegible] Children—

1 W. James, b. May 31, 18[illegible].

Henrietta, b. Feb. 7, 18[illegible], m. N. A. Lafayette [illegible]. Genevieve, b. Sept. 10, 1867. Lives at [illegible] Thirty [illegible]

Martha, b. Apr. [illegible], 18[illegible], m. [illegible] of Great Barrington, M[illegible].

56221[illegible] [illegible] Great Barrington, Mass. [illegible] May 2[illegible] [illegible] N. Y. [illegible]

1 [illegible]

2 [illegible].

3 [illegible]

[illegible]

[illegible]

[illegible]

1 George [illegible]
Mary, m Wm. [illegible] New York [illegible]
2 [illegible]

503 ASA, b [illegible] at [illegible], Ct., m [illegible] of [illegible]
Jan. 12, [illegible] 27, [illegible] March, [illegible] Children—
1 [illegible], b June 17, 1769.
2 Elisha, b July 26, 1771.
3 Bethel, b Jan. 29, 1774.
4 [illegible], b Oct. 14, 1773.
5 Alvin, b Sept. 16, 1779.
6 Artemas, b June 16, 1782.
7 Oliver, b March [illegible], 1785.
Phil[illegible], b Apr. 13, 17[illegible], m Lorin Crocker.
Sarah, b Dec. 28, 1789.

5031 CHANDLER, b in Bozrah, Ct., June 24, 17[illegible], m Feb. 27, 17[illegible], Hannah Hyde Metcalf, who was b June 8, 1771, and d Sept. 27, 1811; for his second wife he m Fanny Hough. He d at Bozrah Aug. 15, 1849. By his 2d wife he had one son.
1 David Chandler, who m Ruth P. Elwin, 1[illegible], and d in Norwich.

5032 ELISHA, b Bozrah, Ct., July 26, 1771, m Mary Harris at Bozrah, Aug. 17, 179[illegible], and for his second wife Catharine Tice; farmer, [illegible], N. Y. Children—
1 [illegible], b Aug. 5, 17[illegible].
2 Daniel, b Oct. 2, 17[illegible].
3 Gilbert, b Oct. 27, 1798.
Mary, b July [illegible]
[illegible], b [illegible], Feb. [illegible]
4 [illegible], b [illegible], 17[illegible], New London.
[illegible] Oct. [illegible] 26, [illegible]
[illegible]
[illegible]

[illegible]

56..21 ASA [illegible] 17 [illegible] Kelloggy [illegible] to Kellogg, [illegible]
1 Charles [illegible]
Rachel A[illegible], d. in infancy.
2 Susan [illegible], d. at age of 31.
3 Horace Rogers
Ann [illegible], unmarried, aged 24.
[illegible] Stedman, [illegible] and [illegible].
Ruth Rogers, [illegible] unmarried, in 1856.
Mary [illegible], d. unmarried.
4 [illegible] Brown.
Isabel, d. at age of 12.
Abby [illegible], b. 1842.
[illegible] Rogers, b. [illegible].
Emma Jane, d. in infancy.
5 Clarence Asa

562211 CHARLES LATHROP, [illegible] at Mystic, Ct.

563213 HORACE ROGERS, m. Jane Snow, settled at [illegible]; had [illegible] children.

562..2 DANIEL, b. [illegible], Ct., Oct. 2, [illegible], m. [illegible] 1830 [illegible] Holmes, [illegible], Ct. She was b. at East Haddam, Ct., March 2 [illegible] and d. at [illegible], Ct., [illegible] 4, 1 [illegible]

563:3 GILES, b. [illegible], Ct., Aug. 2[illegible] 17[illegible], [illegible] Hyde, [illegible] Rev. [illegible] Children—
Angeline C.
Elizabeth A., m. Joseph [illegible] children.
1 William W.
2 Albert [illegible]
3 Samuel [illegible]
Harriet [illegible] Rev. [illegible]
4 [illegible]

[illegible]

[illegible]

[illegible]

1 Joshua Hyde, b. Nov. 1, 1[illegible]

Margaret M[illegible], b. O[illegible] 2[illegible], 18[illegible].

Sally Tracey, b. May 17, 18[illegible] [illegible], N[illegible] W. Long [illegible], b. [illegible] d. A[illegible]

[illegible]31 JOSHUA HYDE, b. at Franklin, Ct., Nov. 1, 18[illegible] [illegible] Olive A. Southworth, settled at [illegible], [illegible] d. July 8, [illegible]

Mary Raymond, b. A[illegible] 10, 1[illegible], d. Sep. 2[illegible], 18[illegible]

56[illegible] NANALA[illegible], b. at [illegible], Ct., Oct. 11, 17[illegible] [illegible] Phelps of Lebanon, lived in Franklin. Children:

1 David Austin.

2 Francis Chandler.

Mary Elizabeth.

5631l DAVID AUSTIN, b. at [illegible], Ct., [illegible] He settled in New York, where he [illegible] for many years a [illegible] publisher, with an office in Barclay street. We are [illegible] for much valuable aid in the preparation of this work. He [illegible] at Oyster Bay, L. I., March, 18[illegible].

56312 FRANCIS CHANDLER, b. at [illegible] [illegible]

[illegible]

[illegible]

[illegible]

[illegible]

[illegible]

[illegible]

[illegible]

[illegible]

[illegible]

And [illegible]

His brother, [illegible] was [illegible] paid [illegible] of [illegible]. He [illegible] recently [illegible] the [illegible] He d Jan. [illegible] 18[illegible], [illegible] from Savannah to New York. Children—

1 Fran [illegible].

Mary.

5635 ALVIN, b at [illegible], Ct., Sept. [illegible] 17[illegible], m Jan. 2[illegible], 1[illegible] at Norwich, Ct., Lorena [illegible], b Feb. [illegible], 17[illegible], [illegible] Norwich. Children—

Elizabeth, b Nov. [illegible], 1[illegible], unmarried.

Lorena, b March 31, 1[illegible].

Alvin Church, d in infancy.

John H., d in [illegible].

Susan, m James Taylor, merchant, Ithaca, N. Y., moved to Oshkosh, Wis.

ALVIN was a [illegible], settled first in [illegible], then in [illegible], Ct., then in [illegible], N. Y., and in 1826 moved to Ithaca. After his wife d, 1[illegible], he d in 1[illegible].

5636 ARTEMAS, b at [illegible], Ct., June 10, 1782, m Nov. 21, 1[illegible], Nancy Hough. They moved to Orangeville, N. Y., where he was killed by accident July 2, [illegible]. Children—

Harriet, m Hyde [illegible] June [illegible], 18[illegible].

[illegible] Wright [illegible] Oct. 2[illegible], 18[illegible].

5637 OLIVER, b at [illegible], March 6, 17[illegible], m Feb. 7, 18[illegible], Sylvia Baldwin, moved to Halifax, Vt., and afterwards to [illegible], Ct. He was a [illegible]. Children—

1 [illegible] Baldwin.

2 [illegible]

Octavia, m Harvey [illegible], Vt.

[illegible]

Rachel [illegible]

Sybil P., m [illegible]

[illegible]

[illegible]

1 [illegible]

2 [illegible]

[illegible] HENRY [illegible], b. [illegible] Waterford, Ct. Children:

Ellis Richards.

1 [illegible] Henry.

Leroy, b. Oct. [illegible] d. Dec. 31, 18[illegible].

[illegible] M., b. [illegible] d. July 9, 18[illegible].

2 [illegible] A., b. at New [illegible], Sept. 12, 18[illegible].

[illegible] NATHAN AVERY, b. Waterford, Ct., 18[illegible], m. Sept. [illegible]

Laura B., b. April 2[illegible], 18[illegible].

164 STEPHEN, b. Nov. 26, 17[illegible], m. Eunice [illegible] of [illegible]. She was b. at Norwich, Aug. 17, 1751.

[illegible]

[illegible]

1 NATHAN [illegible] 1827 [illegible]
[illegible]
1 Addison, [illegible] Ohio.

2 JOHN [illegible] lived and died in [illegible], Vt. Children:
[illegible] Canada.
[illegible] Penn.
1 John.
[illegible] in the [illegible]
New York.
2 George.
3 [illegible]
4 Thompson D.
5 Frederick, [illegible]
[illegible] 2 children, Vt.
[illegible] 5 children, Toledo, Ohio.

21 JOHN, [illegible], Vt. [illegible] Charlotte Sinclair. Children:
1 George W.
2 [illegible]
3 [illegible]
4 [illegible]
5 [illegible]

211 GEORGE W. [illegible], Vt. [illegible] W. [illegible]
[illegible] N. Y.
2 George W.

211 GEORGE W. [illegible], Vt. [illegible]
[illegible]

[illegible] York City.
[illegible]
[illegible]

23 Ward [illegible], 5 children [illegible] in Vt.

24 THOMPSON D., [illegible], m [illegible] Follet, daughter of Judge Follet, [illegible]shire, Vt. Children—

Eliza, m Adam Fleck, Newark, O.

Rosetta, single, Granville, O.

Persis, single, Granville, O.

1 Truman.

241 TRUMAN, dealer in hardware, Carey, Wyandotte Co., O., m Sallie Guntner, of Findlay, O. Children—

1 Truman B., b 1868.

Two other children who d in infancy.

The following family came from an ancestor whose given name is uncertain, but which our informant thinks was Dyer, whose occupation was weaver and who lived in Stonington, Ct. He was probably a descendant of WALTER; but whether he came from Little Compton, Lebanon or Norwich we have no knowledge or "information sufficient to form a belief." Children—

1 William.

2 Oliver.

3 Daniel.

4 Dyer.

4 Nathaniel.

Annie.

11 WILLIAM, b at Stonington, Ct., moved to Coopers Plains, N. Y., m Phebe Adams. Children—

1 Moses.

2 Daniel.

Anna, m Lyman Bisby.

Phebe.

Eunice, m Benjamin Jenkins.

Mary H. G., m ----- French.

Rachel, m Reuben Mather, Middleville, Mich.

111 MOSES, farmer, Coopers Plains, N. Y., m Eliza Hammond. Children—

Olive, m Aaron Quick.

Theresa.

112 DANIEL, b Coopers Plains, N. Y., moved to Illinois, m Mary Woodward. Children—

1 John M., and other children.

[illegible]

12 [illegible]

[illegible]

1 [illegible]

[illegible]

[illegible]

2 [illegible]

122 ISRAEL [illegible]

[illegible]

1 Allen B.

2 [illegible]

3 [illegible]

4 [illegible]

5 [illegible] N. Y., [illegible]

6 [illegible]

7 [illegible]

1221 ALLEN B., [illegible] N. J., m [illegible]

[illegible]

1 Jay B.

1222 LEWIS, farmer, [illegible], N. Y., served three y[illegible] Army during the Rebellion.

4 DANIEL, m Lucy Murray, Suffield, Ct., had one son

1 Lyman A.

41 LYMAN A., m [illegible] Gillett, Suffield, Ct. Children—

1 Chester W.

2 Milton, lives at [illegible] Ct.

3 Mary, m Henry Chamberlain, Hartford, Ct.

4 Lucy, m [illegible] Bradley.

411 CHESTER W., [illegible], Suffield, Ct., m Mary A. Sh[illegible].

1 Thomas W.

2 Albert [illegible]

3 Susan Elizabeth

4 Mary [illegible].

[illegible] B. W[illegible] of Lowell, Mass., who is in the lumber business says of it: "His invention wrought a great revolution in the mechanical world, doing more than any other probably to develop the great industries dependent on lumber, which I think ranks third on the list of all the great material interests of the country; and judging its utility to mankind by its results, which it may be granted are of less magnitude than those achieved by Watt, Fulton, Stephenson and Morse, are nevertheless of such vast proportions as to entitle the originator of the cylinder planing machine to a position in the front rank of the great inventors of the age." WILLIAM obtained his patent from the Government Dec. 27, 1828. There was a great deal of litigation over it and his rights as patentee were not fully established until after his death. For further particulars regarding this litigation, see 4 Howard's U. S. Supreme Court Reports, p 646. Wm. died in New York City Feb. 3. 1839, and letters of administration were granted to his son, William. He left the following children—

Almira S.
Charlotte S., m —— Everts.
1 William W.

WILLIAM W., lived at Hyde Park for several years after his father's death, and continued the litigations over the planing machine patent to their final success. He was Supervisor of the town in 1843. He afterwards settled in Yonkers, N. Y., where he went largely into real estate speculations, which for a time were successful, but finally resulted disastrously to him. He m Sophia L. —— and d Feb. 13, 1873, at Yonkers. Children—

Ada S., m —— Ferris, Philadelphia.
1 Charles R.
Gertrude E., m —— Miles, Philadelphia.
Mary K. W.
2 James G.
3 Atherton.
4 Washington.
Henrietta.
5 William V.

I find in the Roster of State Troops a William, who was Lieutenant in the 6th Regt. from Dutchess Co., Col. David Sutherland; promoted to be 1st Lieutenant March 22, 1776. He may have been William, the inventor.

The following family is of such high character that it is to be

r[illegible] the [illegible] which [illegible] connects [illegible] the family of WALTER of S[illegible], has not yet been discovered.

WILLIAM, b at Old [illegible], Ct., [illegible] 4, 17[illegible]; moved with his parents in 1745 to Cambridge, Washington Co., N. Y. He served in the Revolutionary War as First Lieutenant in the 16th Cambridge Regiment, Col. Lewis Van Woert. He was with Gen. Stark in his operations against Burgoyne, and with Gen. Gates at Saratoga in 1777. William is said to have had a brother Ephraim, who settled in Saratoga Co., and who was a Captain in the 13th Regiment, Albany Co. militia, and served four months in 1779. Ephraim's son Ephraim also served as private in the same regiment. WILLIAM m Mary Lott Nov. 18, 1761. His farm was about a mile and a half east of Cambridge Village, in what is now White Creek. His children all b at Cambridge were--

Sarah, b Aug. 20, 1764.
1 Lott, b May 21, 1766.
2 William, b Feb. 8, 1768.
Mary, b April 1, 1769.
Rosannah, b Jan. 1, 1771.
Esther, b Nov. 8, 1773.
Hannah, b March 17, 1775.
3 Gershom, b Nov. 17, 1776.
Charity, b Jan. 16, 1780.
Elizabeth, b Nov. 13, 1781.
Freelove, b July 26, 1783.
Jane, b April 29, 1785.

1 LOTT, b at Cambridge, N. Y., May 21, 1766; occupation, woolen manufacturer. He was a Major of militia and served at the battle of Plattsburg in 1814. He d about 1840. His wife Asenath Heth, b Nov. 13, 1768, d in 1851. Children all b at Cambridge

Mary, b Aug. 25, 1787, m D. P. Wright, Oswego Co., N. Y.
Asenath, b March 18, 1789, m —— Sharp, Cambridge.
1 Lott, b Sept. 16, 1791.
2 Ira, b Sept. 17, 1793.
Anna, b Nov. 15, 1795, m Francis Crocker, Fairfax Co., Va.
Orra, b April 23, 1799, m John Simpson, Springfield, Mich.
3 William, b June 5, 1805.
4 Calvin Van Kirk, b Sept. 22, 1807.

11 LOTT, b at Cambridge, N. Y., m and settled in Washington Co., and had a large family.

12 IRA, b at Cambridge, N. Y., Sept. 17, 1793; lived in Washington Co., had a large family.

13 WILLIAM, b at Cambridge, N. Y., June 5, 18[illegible], farmer; resided in Oswego Co., N. Y.; Fairfax Co., Va., and at Westfield, Ind., where he d March 11, 1867. He m Sharley Gilbert Norton 1830; she d at Westfield, Oct. 22, 18[illegible]. Children—

Harriet Norton, b March [illegible], 1837, m Dr. J. Pettijohn, Westfield, Ind.

1 Milton, b Sept. 21, 1834, m in Washington, D. C.; has one child, George.

Mary Asenath, b July 12, 1843, d July 22, 1867, unmarried.

1 Malcolm William, b Jan. 31, 1832.

131 MALCOLM WILLIAM, b in Oswego Co., N. Y., Jan. 31, 1832; has been for many years pastor of the Presbyterian Church, Burlington, W. Va.; married (1) Susan E. Streit May 5, 1864; (2) Isabella J. Raymond Sept. 22, 1881. Children—

1 William Streit, b Dec. 17, 1865.

2 Robert Bell, b April 25, 1868.

Nannie Bell, b Feb. 28, 1870.

3 Malcolm Graham, b Feb. 28, 1870.

Mary Moore, b Oct. 27, 1872.

4 James Finley, b July 21, 1876, d Jan. 15, 1881.

14 CALVIN VAN KIRK, b Sept. 22, 1807, at Cambridge, N. Y., farmer, m Dolly Fitch Dec. 4, 1833; Janette Fenwick June 10, 1848, and Kate Clapp March 20, 1873. Calvin moved to Fairfax Co., Va., in 1851, and again after a few years to Steuben Co., N. Y. Children—

Harriet, b July 26, 1832, m —— Ashton, Washington Co., N. Y.

1 Samuel Fitch, b June 27, 1834.

Sarah Ann, b May 30, 1836.

2 Henry Patterson, b June 21, 1838.

Julia, b Feb. 29, 1840.

Maria Boid, b Nov. 1, 1841.

Dolly Mary, b April 11, 1847.

3 William, b Oct. 18, 1848.

4 Marvin, b April 16, 1850.

Eunice Amelia, b June 6, 1852.

Anna Jennette, b July 12, 1854.

6 Alexander B., b Dec. 22, 1857.

5 Calvin Van Kirk, b Jan. 1 1856.

Asenath Lott, b March 4, 1860.

145 CALVIN VAN KIRK, b Jan. 1, 1856, m Hattie L. Bingham Feb. 17, 1886; is in the hardware business at Kiowa, Kansas.

[illegible]
[illegible] Aurelius, Cayuga Co., N. Y., [illegible] Oct. [illegible], 1825, Julius C. Strong, clothing merchant, at Waterloo N. Y.

During the latter half of the last century quite a number of Woodworths from Lebanon and Norwich settled independently of each other in Vermont. Nathan (5??) went to Wells; and I find in Paul's History of Wells the following names: Roswell, m Amanda, daughter of Nathan Francis, and settled on the farm now (1869) owned by Nelson Lewis. He was in Capt. Ebenezer Green's Co., Col. Bedel's Regiment in 1776. He had the following children: Betsey, m Daniel Hulett, Paulet, Vt.; Harmony m Joshua Hulett, of Paulet, Josiah, Downer, Roswell, Sally, Sophronia, m James Francis; Louisa, Patty, Samuel, Charles, Socrates. Roswell, Sr., went West in 1816, and all further trace of his family is lost.
JOSEPH (5322) settled at Onion River, Vt., soon after the Revolution, and his brother ZIBA (5323) bought lands and settled in Montpelier, Vt.

There was an ABEL living in Norwich, Windsor Co., Vt., about 1800, who m Olive Partridge and had nine children: Laura, Sarah, Lucinda H., Harriet, Olivia, Mary Jane, Hiram Partridge, Leonard Hartwell, Benjamin Paschal and Cyrus S.
LEONARD HARTWELL, son of ABEL, lived at Rock Falls, Whiteside Co., Ill; married and had the following children: May, b Feb. 28, 1842, d Jan. 29, 1844; Andrew Sullivan, b Jan. 22, 1844, m Jan. 12, 1875; Cyrus Clarence, b Oct. 22, 1852, m June 13, 1878; Sarah, b June 12, 1855, m Nov. 27, 1878, John H. Montague.
CYRUS S., son of ABEL, b at Norwich, Vt., June 11, 1819, m Jan. 7 1858, Sarah Buckingham, b at Norwalk, O., June 8, 1838. CYRUS S. lives at Salem, Marion Co., Oregon, where he is agent for the Oregon Railway and Navigation Co. Children—
1 William Griswold, b July 16, 1859, lives at Portland, Oregon.
2 Cyrus Buckingham, b Jan. 26, 1861, bank teller, Salem, Oregon, m Kate Lincoln Applegate May 14, 1884; has one son, Cyrus Applegate, b at Portland, Oregon, July 11, 1885.

There was a TIMOTHY living after the Revolution at Royalton, Vt., who m a Fowler. He had considerable local reputation as an athlete and later in life applied his "muscular Christianity" to the ministry of the gospel. Children—
1 Lyman.

2 William.
Polly, Sarah and another.

1 LYMAN, farmer, lived at Strafford, Vt., m Mary Preston. Children—
Louisa.
Lyman W., d.
Mary Ann.
Rhoda W., d.
1 Alexander Preston, b July 20, 1822.
Lucy.
2 Wilbur Fisk.
Walter Felton, d.
Ellen B.

11 ALEXANDER PRESTON, b at Strafford, Vt., July 20, 1822, farmer, South Turnbridge, Vt., m Matilda Felton, b at Turnbridge, July 2, 1833. Children—
1 Charles Lyman, b June 19, 1856.
2 William A., b July 11, 1858.
Flora E., d.
Effie J., b May 20, 1868, graduate of Normal School, Randolph, Vt., is now a teacher.

111 CHARLES LYMAN, b June 19, 1856, at Turnbridge' Vt., station agent, Wabash, Dakota; m (1) Annie Laurie Cary, of Sherburn, N. Y., Oct. 19, 1880; (2) Addie Hall, Cadyville, N. Y.; has one son, Robert Hall, b Jan. 12, 1885.

112 WILLIAM A., b July 11, 1858; teacher of phonography, etc., at Eastman's Business College, Poughkeepsie, N. Y.; moved later to Denver, Col.; married Louisa S. Black, of South Royalton, Vt., Dec. 8, 1880; has one son, Ivanhoe W.

12 WILBUR FISK, physician, settled in Michigan, where he was at one time a Probate Judge and later in Kansas, where he was a State Senator. At last accounts he was connected with the Medical College at Indianapolis, Ind.; has two sons, one named Archer living in Chicago.

2 WILLIAM, son of Timothy, had a son Albert, who had five children: Francis, Frederick and others.

JABEZ (22316) moved from Dorchester, N. H., to Essex Co., Vt., with one or two of his brothers, and there reared a large family from whom probably many of the Vermont families have sprung, though it has not been possible as yet to trace the connections.

From the town records of Scituate I take the following names, which do not appear in the foregoing pages and of which I have no further trace:

Ebenezer Woodworth, son of Martha Woodworth, alias Martha Right, was born April 1[illegible], 170[illegible].
Ebenezer Woodworth married Hannah Woodworth, March 20, 1713
Hannah Woodworth, m Samuel Jackson Oct. 20, 1715.
Hannah Woodworth, m Jacob Lincoln Aug. 2, 1770.
Robert Woodworth, m Mary Soper Sept. 11, 1735.
Mollie Woodworth, m John Rice Feb. 2, 1769.

From Little Compton records:

William Woodworth, m Eliza Carver April 6, 1825.
Robert W. Woodworth, of Newport, son of William Woodworth, deceased, and Martha, his wife, and Delaney, daughter of Phillip Dring and Ruth, his wife, were married Feb. 27, 1876.
From Lebanon Church records.--The dates represent probably either dates of baptisms or of admission to membership:
Caleb, 1704. Clemence, 1711-1716. Benjamin, 1707. Hannah, 1707. Joseph, 1743. Joseph, 1745. Amy, 1746. Elisha, 1749. Keziah, 1756. Rachel, 1757. Asael, 1760. Heman, 1762. Eunice, 1770. Lucy, 1772. Betsey, 1797. Jeduthon, 1764. Walter, 1766. Eunice, 1770. Olive, 1770.

Marriages--

Mary Woodworth, m Benjamin Sprague Dec. 29, 1707.
Lydia Woodworth, m Lemuel Cleveland Nov. 5, 1745.
Benjamin Woodworth, m Katherine Shelds June 18, 1756.
Benjamin Woodworth, m Mary Marsh, 1744.
William Woodworth, m Ann Symns Aug. 6, 1760.

Deaths--

Widow Anne Woodworth d July 12, 1789, aged 83.
Benjamin Woodworth d Aug., 1828, aged about 65.
From Church records, Old Norwich Town--
Hannah Woodworth, m Benjamin Palmer Nov. 28, 1811.
Catharine Woodworth, m ---- Bennett Oct. 24, 1790.
Betsey Woodworth, m Elie Adams Nov. 5, 1794.
Franklin was set off from Norwich as a separate town in 1786. I gather the following from church and town records:
Harvey Woodworth, of Coventry, m Eliza Roberts, of Hartford, at Franklin, Nov. 5, 1815.

Mary [illegible] Moler April 5, 1855
Anna [illegible] 1774 to Asa [illegible].
David C. Woodworth registered as elector, 1840.
Charles L. Woodworth registered as elector, 1844.
George H. Woodworth registered as elector, 1852.
Waterman C. Woodworth registered as elector 1858.
Sarah, widow of Asa Woodworth, died April 2, 1861, aged 82.
Nabby joined the church by profession, June 4, 1798.
Mary Stedman joined the church by profession June 28, 1801.
Melinda joined the church by profession Sept. 2, 1803.
Vera Ann joined the church by profession July 4, 1806.
George Burch joined the church by profession Dec. 30, 1814.
Ezra m Elizabeth Reber, Oct. 17, 1821.
Caroline P. m George W. Loomis Nov. 12, 1854.
Edward B., Concord, N. H. m Helen M. Whiton Sept. 9, 1875.

From Norwich records.

Charles E. Woodworth, m Mary E. Harrington, March 2, 1845.
John F. Woodworth, of New York, m Sarah F. Winship Feb. 7, 1841.
Oliver Woodworth, m Eliphal, daughter of Capt. Richard Cook, who d 1795. Eliphal d Jan. 25, 1842, aged 92. Oliver, deacon in Greenville Church, d Feb. 7, 1865, aged 71.

From the town records of Salisbury, Conn., I extract the following items:
In 1739 Caleb Woodworth purchased from Thomas Newcomb 100 acres of land in Salisbury. In 1758 Caleb is appointed Surveyor of Roads, and in 1764 there is filed a certificate showing that he contributed to the Baptist Church at Oblong. It appears that his wife's name was Jane and that he had three sons, one of whom at least was born at Salisbury. There may have been other children, some perhaps born in Lebanon. The following are the only children of which we have at present any knowledge—
1 Caleb.
2 Cyrenus.
3 Solomon, b May 4, 1848.

CALEB probably moved to Montgomery Co., where he was a delegate to the General Convention held there in 1801.

CYRENUS, m Abigail ----, at Salisbury. Children—
Abigail, b July 15, 1762.
1 Samuel, b Aug. 20, 1763.

2 Cyrenus, b June 28, 1766.
3 Josiah, b Nov. 10, 1768.
4 Luke, b Aug. 10, 1771.
5 Luther, b Nov. 25, 1773.
6 Darius, b Nov. 23, 1775.
7 James, b Oct. 24, 1778.
8 Joel, b June 3, 1783.

21 SAMUEL, b at Salisbury July 15, 1762; sold his dwelling house in 1799 to Joseph Johnson for $40.

22 CYRENUS, b at Salisbury, June 25, 1766; no further trace.

23 JOSIAH sold his dwelling house in 1799 to Darius Woodworth for $160. May 10, 1806, his father conveys to Josiah by deed all his lands received from his father Caleb. In 1811. Josiah bought land of Samuel Langdon for $160. Josiah was taxed in 1815 for $141.03.

24 LUKE, b at Salisbury, Aug. 10, 1771. m Jane ———. Children—
Sally, b July 31, 1791.
Abigail, b July 3, 1793.

26 DARIUS, b Nov. 23, 1775. m Hannah ———. Children—
Clarissa, b Jan. 30, 1791.

27 JAMES and Luther lived together at Salisbury until 1815 when they sold their house. James m Helen Pattison; had one son—Henry, b July 1, 1815; died at Salisbury, Aug. 8, 1887.

3 SOLOMON, b at Salisbury, May 4 1748 m Phebe Thornton, Oct. 18. 1770, had one son—
Caleb, b April 7. 1771, d April 13, 1771.

I also find the following family mentioned in the Salisbury records:

Ephraim whose wife's name was Anna had the following children b at Salisbury—
Anna, b Mar. 30, 1755, d April 12, 1755.
1 Ephraim, b March, — —.
Jerusha, b April 17, 1758.

I have received from Mr. H. B. Child, of 7 East 77th St., N. Y., a continuation of the account of Ephraim's descendants.

CAPTAIN EPHRAIM WOODWORTH was born about 1732 at Connecticut. Ancestors and nativity unknown. Among his brothers is supposed to be the WILLIAM who lived in 1776 in the Charlotte Precinct of Dutchess Co., N. Y. Judge Gibson, of Salem, is a de-

[illegible] of this line. [illegible] her brother is thought to have been Robert, of Schenectady, below Albany, father of the distinguished Judge, John Woodworth, b [illegible], d 18[illegible]. Capt. Ephraim Woodworth in about the year 17[illegible] married ANNA MOORE, daughter of Jonathan Moore, of Salisbury, formerly of Simsbury, Conn., and

HANNAH LONG, daughter of Thomas Long, of Hartford Ct.

Anna Moore's sister, Abigail Moore, m Philip Spencer (1751) and they became the mother and father of Hon. Ambrose Spencer (b 1758). Judge Ambrose Spencer was the brother-in-law of Gov. DeWitt Clinton and Capt. Ephraim Woodworth was the uncle of Judge Ambrose Spencer.

Anna Moore's mother, Hannah Long, was daughter of Thomas Long, who married Sarah Wilcox, daughter and only child of John Wilcox, of Hartford, and afterwards of Middletown by his first wife, Sarah Wadsworth, the daughter of William Wadsworth, Esq., one of the first settlers of Hartford. Ancestor of the Rev. Daniel Wadsworth, of Hartford, and Col. Jeremiah and Daniel Wadsworth, Gen. William Wadsworth and Hon. James Wadsworth, of Genesee, N. Y., and of a long line of distinguished men of this name.

See "Goodwin's Genealogical Notes of First Settlers of Conn. and Mass.," pp. 310-320, and "Phelp's History of Simsbury, Ct." 171, for accounts of the Spencer, Moore, Long, and Wadsworth families.

Of Capt. Ephraim and Anna Moore Woodworth's children there were—

Anna, b Salisbury, Ct., March 30, 1755, d April 12, 1755.

Ephraim, Jr., b at Salisbury, Ct., April 2, 1756, m Delight Rowley, d March 5, 1838, at Bemis Heights, Saratoga Co., N. Y.; a Revolutionary soldier.

Jerusha, b April 17, 1758, at Salisbury, Ct., m —— Hart.

Reuben, a Revolutionary soldier and Major in War of 1812, 41st Regiment.

Isaac.

James.

Mary, b Feb. 2, 1771, m Dr. Ephraim Child Jan. 1, 1793 (see infra).

Anna, who m Nehemiah Moody, a Captain in the Revolution also.

Charlotte, m —— Hart.

Capt. Ephraim Woodworth, before the Revolution, removed with his family to the town of Stillwater, Saratoga Co., N. Y., and was a man of considerable influence and prominence. He became Capt.

[illegible] the Fourth Co., [illegible] N. Y. Militia, under Col. [illegible] McCrea, and fought through the battles at Saratoga and the war. His sons, Ephraim, Jr., and Reuben, and Amos Woodworth were in his company.

See N. Y. State Archives 271. His house was the headquarters of Gen. Gates. He was a farmer and a weaver, and the hospital of the battle was his shop.
See Sylvester's History of Saratoga Co., pp 90, 280, 306 for interesting account. He d 1825 at Northumberland (next town to Stillwater), Saratoga Co., N. Y.; left will dated Oct. 8, 1818, Bk. Wills, 6, p. 396.

MARY MOORE WOODWORTH, youngest child and daughter of Capt. Ephraim and Anna Moore Woodworth, was born Feb. 2, 1751, at Stillwater, N. Y., and d at Syracuse, N. Y., July 18, 1843. She m Jan. 1, 1796, Dr. Ephraim Child, of Stillwater, N. Y., son of Capt. Increase Child, of Woodstock, Ct.; Capt. in the Revolution and a soldier under Gen. Putnam in the French and English wars of 1755-8, and a lineal descendant of Ephraim and Benjamin Child, who emigrated to this country in 1630 with Gov Winthrop and settled at Roxbury, Mass. Dr. Child was surgeon of the 41st Regiment, War of 1812, and one of the founders of the Saratoga County Medical Society, and d June 10th, 1830, at Stillwater. They had ten children, among them Orville Woodworth Childs, the eminent engineer. Noadiah Moody Childs, a prominent citizen of Syracuse, N. Y., father of Daniel Brewer Childs.
See Child's Genealogy, pp 117, 119, 125.
The next three items from the Salisbury records are interesting from the similarity of names to those mentioned by Dorris A. Woodworth and the venerable W. G., on page 62 as belonging to their ancestors. It is quite likely that the family of Dorris A. came from Salisbury and is related to Ephraim and perhaps Caleb.
Gershom Woodworth m Roxanna Everts Nov. 21, 1749. They may be the parents of Gershom Everts.
Selah Woodworth m Rebeccah Dunham, of Sheffield.
Freelove m Jesse Chatfield Oct. 18, 1756. Wm. G. says Freelove m a Canfield. These names are near enough alike to allow for a lapse of memory on the part of our aged contributor.

Other names on Salisbury records are:

Sarah Woodworth m J. Canfield Dec. 2, 1761.
Mary Woodworth m Levi Benton Oct. 29, 1769.

Theodore Woodworth, m Sarah —— April 13, 18[illegible]8.

Theodore Woodworth, of Ellenville, m Maria Silvernail, of Salisbury, Oct., 1828.

Henry, of N. E., N. Y., m Sally Ann Reed June 12, 1842.

Hannah Maria m Edmund Lat[illegible]on Nov. 10, 18[illegible].

Mary, of Danbury, age 74, m Nathaniel Store, age 67, Feb. 16, 1851.

Jesse, of Montville, age 53, m Mary A. Preston 185 .

Abigail, age 26, m Mortimer Chapman, of Newburg, 185 .

James, age 26, of N. E., N. Y., m B---- S---- Aug. 14, 1881.

Jennie S., age 22, m Frank S. Williams, Mowerpe, Ill., Aug. 9, 1883.

Maldie, age 23, m M. A. Sparks Sept. 30, 1891.

An infant son of Jesse and Fanny Woodworth d March 30, 1856.

There was a George Woodworth, b Feb. 17, 1802, at Norwich, Ct.; d March 8, 1864, at Hampton, Conn., whose mother's name was Clara Aspinwall, but whose father's name is unknown.

George m Sept. 25, 1824, at Scotland, Ct., Marcia Learned. (See Learned genealogy.) Children—

Harriet Newell, b May 25, 1825, m (1) John P. Barnett, (2) Newton S. Clark; she d Aug. 28, 1896.

Mary Learned, b Sept. 21, 1828, m (1) Lyman Greenslet, (2) Elijah Button; d July 17, 1886.

Marcia, b March 10, 1832, m (1) Joseph E. Houde, (2) Henry E. Thompson.

Emily b Feb. 23, 1837, m (1) Joseph Troye, (2) Fredk Taylor, d Dec. 23, 1884.

Emma, b Feb. 23, 1837, m Nov. 29, 1859, Wm Henry Lincoln.

The following family I am unable to connect with that of Walter Woodworth:

SAMUEL WOODWORTH had two sons—

1 Samuel.

2 Daniel.

1 DANIEL had a son—

1 Samuel, b May 27, 1800.

2 Charles, b 1805.

11 SAMUEL, b May 27, 1800, farmer, Yorkshire, N. Y., m Feb. 27, 1823, Annette Whitney, daughter of Palmer Whitney, of Warwick, Mass. Samuel d Feb. 4, 1863. Children—

Minerva, b July 1, 1824, m Aug., 1842, David C. Wooley; d May 7, 1892.

Celia, b Nov. 30, 1826, d Jan. 18, 1827.

1 Harry E., b [illegible]
2 Charles, b Aug. 27, [illegible] d Jan. 29, 1843.
Anna Maria, b Oct. 15, 1836, m Jan. 22, 1857, Brayton B. [illegible]; lives at Richmondville, Sanilac Co., Mich.
Nancy Aseneth, b Nov. 12, 1839, m Feb. 11, 1861; Gordon Parker; lives at Wales, Erie Co., N. Y.
3 Samuel Parker, b Sept. 5, 1842, d Oct. 31, 1865.

111 HARRY E., b Feb. 4, 1825, m Sept. 12, 1850, Elvira Blood; resided at Java, N. Y., Groton, Tompkins Co., N. Y., and Delavan, Cattaraugus Co., N. Y.

12 CHARLES, b about 1805, m Nancy W. Whitney; had a daughter, Emily, m —— Twiss, Aurora, N. Y.
1 Henry L., m Lucia Brown, Bloomingdale, N. Y.

2 DANIEL, m Bathsheba Gardner and lived at Yorkshire, Cattaraugus Co., N. Y. He was a farmer. Children—
1 Daniel, b 1802.
2 Harry.

21 DANIEL, b 1802, in Fenner, Madison Co., N. Y., farmer, m Nancy Dairs; had seven children—
1 Delos D., b 1827.
N. Lucretia, b 1829, m Silas Clough, Arcade, Wyoming Co., N. Y.
1 Eli D., b 1832.
3 Charles A., b 1835.
Louisa R., b 1837, d 1857.
4 Dwight S., b 1840.
5 Judson M., b 1843.

211 DELOS D., b 1827, m —— Clough; was a Baptist minister; settled in Busti, Chautauqua Co., N. Y.; d 1860; one child—
Ada Bell, m.

212 ELI D., b 1832, physician, Eagle, Wyoming Co., N. Y., m —— Shields; has one child, b 1876.

213 CHARLES A., Methodist minister, m —— Smith; settled in 1883 at Genesee, Livingston Co., N. Y. Children—
1 Daniel.
2 Charles.
Evangeline
Emma.
3 William.

214 DWIGHT [illegible] secretary [illegible] Mutual A [illegible] Accident Association, 442 Powers Building, Rochester, N. Y., m Eliza Woodruff. Children—

Carl, d aged 15 years.

1 Frank, b 18[illegible], at Rochester.

215 JUDSON M., b 1843; with the Building & Loan Association, 285 Hudson street, Buffalo; m. 1865, D. A. Fuller at Yorkshire, N. Y. Children—

1 Earl, b 1868.

2 Leon, b 1874.

22 HARRY, lived at Fenner, Madison Co., N. Y., m —— Hutchinson; had one son—

1 D. Melvin, who is m and has ten children.

The following WOODWORTHS were soldiers in the Revolutionary War from Connecticut—

Abel, a privateer on the ship "Oliver Cromwell."

Amasa, private.

Asa, a member of "The Grenadiers."

Asahel, at battle of White Plains, 1776.

Asel, private, wounded at Groton.

Benjamin. There were five Benjamins, one was a drummer and one in "The Grenadiers."

Caleb, from Windham, private.

Charles, from Norwich, private.

Cyrus, Lebanon.

Darius, Norwich.

Dyer.

Eleazur.

Elisha, private 8th Regiment.

Jabez.

Jedediah, Lebanon.

Jesse, Grenadiers.

Jonathan, Sergeant Gen. Putnam's Regiment.

Jonathan, 2d Lieutenant Col. Benedict Arnold's Regiment.

Joseph, private.

Josiah Lebanon, farmer, 5 ft. 6 in. in height, dark gray eyes, black hair.

Recompense, fifer.

[illegible]

[illegible]

[illegible]

Samuel, [illegible] shoemaker, height 5 ft. 10 in., black hair and eyes.

Stephen, Salisbury.

Stephen.

Swift.

Thomas, wounded at Groton.

Timothy.

Walter, in battle of White Plains.

William, corp. Bristol, wounded at Monmouth, N. J.

Ziba, wounded at Groton.

Revolutionary Soldiers from New York State—

NAME.	RANK.	REGIMENT.	COMPANY.
Abel	Private	Whiting	Salisbury.
Amos	"	Van Vechten	Woodman.
Caleb	"	Van Woert	Wells.
Caleb	"	"	Gilman.
Caleb	"	"	Pettit.
Daniel	"	Pawling	Burnett.
Ephraim	"	Van Vechten	Woodworth.
Ephraim, Jr.	"	"	"
Ephraim	Captain	"	"
Gershom	Private	Yates	Brown.
Gershom	Sergeant	"	"
Gershom	Private	Van Woert	Pettit.
Gershom	Lieutenant	"	Wells.
Gershom	"	"	Gilman.
Josiah	Private	"	Wells.
Josiah	"	"	Pettit.
Joshua	"	Gansevoort	De Witt.
Reuben	Drummer	———	———
Robert	Captain	Van Rensselaer	———
Reynol	Private	Brown	Ely.
Salah	Sergeant	Fisher	Little.
Seeley	Private	"	Degrass.
Solomon	"	"	"
Solomon	Lieutenant	Harper	Putnam.
Solomon	"	Fisher	Little.
Solomon	"	Willet	Skinner.
William	Sergeant	Van Woert	Wells.
William	Lieutenant	"	"

INDEX TO CHRISTIAN NAMES OF WOODWORTHS.

[The figures refer to the page.]

A

B

C

D

E

F

G

H

I

J

K

L

M

R

S

T

U

V

W

Z

INDEX TO SURNAMES OTHER THAN WOODWORTH.

A.

B

C

D

E

F

G

H

I

J

K

L

M

N

U

V

W

Y

www.ingramcontent.com/pod-product-compliance
Lightning Source LLC
Chambersburg PA
CBHW031333070726
47496CB00018B/1831